❧

Where
I Am
Now

Also by Robert Day

where
I am
now

stories

robert day

BkMk Press
University of Missouri-Kansas City
5101 Rockhill Road
Kansas City, Missouri 64110
(816) 235-2558
www.umkc.edu/bkmk

Missouri
Arts Council
The State of the Arts

Financial assistance for this project was provided by
the Missouri Arts Council, a state agency.

Cover art: Kathryn Jankus Day
Cover and Book Design: James Dissette
Executive Editor: Robert Stewart
Managing Editor: Ben Furnish
Assistant Managing Editor: Susan L. Schurman
Editorial Assistant: Linda D. Brennaman

BkMk Press wishes to thank Claire Brankin, Brittany L. Coleman,
Ben Hlavacek.

Library of Congress Cataloging-in-Publication Data

Day, Robert
  Where I am now : stories / Robert Day.
      p. cm.
  ISBN 978-1-886157-82-8 (pbk. : alk. paper) 1. Kansas--Fiction. I. Title.
PS3554.A966W47 2012
813'.54--dc23
                              2012028747
ISBN 978-1-886157-82-8

Printing by Walsworth Publishing Co., Marceline, Missouri.

This book is set in Dante MT, Adobe Wood Type Ornaments, Minion Pro.

CONTENTS

Acknowledgments

Thanks to the previous publications in which these stories previously appeared:

"My Father Swims His Horse at Last" from *TriQuarterly*
"Pan-Kansas Swimming Champion" from *Kansas Quarterly*
"The Cold War in Kansas," originally published as "Some Notes on the Cold War in Kansas," *New Letters*
"The One-Man Woodcutter" from *North Dakota Quarterly*
"The Skull Hunter" from *New Letters*
"Where I Am Now" from *New Letters*
"Words Make a Life," *Little Balkans Review*

*This book is for Howard Lamar ,
Tim Seldes, and William Harrison
and is dedicated to Kathryn Jankus Day*

Preface

An editor of mine once commented that first person narratives are like short basketball players. If they are quick and have a good outside shot, they will get their time on the court. If not, not. However it is the third person narratives that are the tall players: in the end they are able to tell the big stories. All the stories in this collection are first person.

The reason my muse and I like first person stories is because together we can be more than ourselves as we tell them. It is as if we are creating a talking family, some of us from one generation and some from another, some adopted, some of dubious parentage. Of course the third person writer can do much the same thing, but not quite. Where you have a narrator, he or she gets both a voice (of course), but also a way of telling a story. Huck Finn has a better way than Mark Twain.

These stories were written over the previous twenty years and are a selection from about the same number of stories that I wrote during those two decades. Reading them over (to correct some wacko mistakes in syntax and fact) I am struck by how much my narrators tell the same story in different ways: stories of loss, stories observed, stories of stories, stories with something unsaid at their core. It is as if they all have the same author.

A few years ago I was walking through the college campus where I teach and came upon two African American boys shooting baskets. I had once played basketball (as a short, slow guard, albeit one with what a coach once called an ICBM range of a jump shot) so I asked the kids for the ball and from more than a modest distance out, drilled nothing but net.

"You know who I am?" I asked as I took another shot and hit it as well.

"No," said one of the boys.

"I'm Michael Jordan."

"No, you're not," the other boy said, this time keeping the ball.

"What makes you think I'm not Michael Jordan?"

"Because," said the first boy, "you're short, old, and fat."

It is what he did not say about my appearance that I like about this story.

Robert Day

My Father Swims His Horse at Last

Verbena

In fact Verbena was not my father's horse but my mother's horse, and by the time my father got around to swimming her across the Big Pond a few years ago, both Verbena and my father were getting old, "long in the tooth, long in the tooth," as my father was fond of saying in his repetitive way and with his life-long affection for things wizened and cranky, a kind of self-affection, now that I think of it. Given my father's spectacular case of procrastination—something he also cherished—it was remarkable that the swim took place at all.

"I'm going to swim the horse this year," my father would say in his annual autumn phone calls to me. "You come back and I'll teach you a few things about swimming horses you might need to know—even if you are a vice president of some business that makes its money off the raw, red backs of the working poor." My father was a dusty and battered High Plains Populist, probably one or two beyond the last of a dead breed, and his concern for the raw, red backs of the working poor permeated his life—as did his hostility toward business vice presidents.

"I am not a vice president," I'd say, something my father knew very well. I sell mortgage insurance. Badly, as it has turned out. Still, my father didn't approve of my job—no matter how poorly I did it, nor with what little conviction. After I graduated from college, he had wanted me to return to the ranch to raise the low-dollar steers we'd buy at auction in the spring to sell off in the fall, never making much money in the process—not that making money ever seemed the point to my father. But more than work, I think he wanted me around for talk.

"Tell me what profit is," my father once said to me in his rhetorical way over supper. Before I could answer he said, "It's time turned into money. Now what do you think of a system of human endeavor that turns time into money?" As a young boy I usually didn't know what to think of my father's opinions.

"What madness is it?" he went on, his John Brown beard jumping with a frustration it has taken me a very long time to appreciate. "What madness is it?" he said. "Tell me, son. Tell me. What madness is it?"

I could not, of course, tell my father what madness it was. But I did vaguely understand, even then, that the phrase was to be one of the several refrains of our lives: What madness is it? The use and beauty of work. Where is Sockless Jerry Simpson (a Populist, like my father) when we need him? Language is life. Time. Your poor, dead mother. Time.

"Time," my father continued after a few minutes, and with some walking about the kitchen to calm down. "Time. Contemplate it, son. Muse on it. Watch it stretch out before you like a long afternoon down by the Big Pond. Look at the Russian olives on the dam wave back and forth through it. Time: See how gossamer a thing it is." Here my father paused and drifted into a detached look, the skin below his eyes bunching up and the point of his beard dropping toward his chest. It seemed as if he was looking through me to find mother, and when he failed, his head would shiver slightly, and that would start him talking again. "Do you know what gossamer means?"

"No." I said.

"Well, it isn't something you'd want to turn into money, now is it?"

Some sons learn to agree with their fathers when they are angry; I learned to agree with my father when for a moment he grew distant. But my father was not distant the last time he called about swimming the horse; he was buoyant.

"You coming back to watch me swim the Big Pond with Verbena, or don't you think you can learn anything from your father anymore?" I sensed a grin behind the gathering hair of his winter beard, a beard he would not trim between the first of September and the first of May.

"I'll be there," I said. "I'll learn what I can about swimming a horse."

"You'll learn more about life from swimming a horse than you can from clipping coupons or figuring interest on your CDs," he said.

"I don't clip coupons," I said. "I don't have CDs."

"No, but I'll bet your bank has neon signs that advertises its money market rates," he said.

"It does," I said. "You have those in Hays as well."

"I expect we do," he said. "That's what we need: the perpetual instruction of the youth about interest rates: Six-point-three-nine percent with a yield of seven-point-two percent. Material madness."

"It's pretty harmless given today's youth," I said.

"It's not harmless to rot their minds so nothing of use or beauty can grow," he said. I could tell the grin was going and my father was about to go *around the bend in the river*—a phrase my mother apparently used to describe my father's quick turns of mood on matters political.

"Better the young should read Jack London," my father went on. "Study the *Iron Heel*. That's use and beauty in a book. Peruse the *US Farm News*. Peace, Parity and Power to the People. Let the youth memorize that."

"We live in a capitalist country," I said.

"Don't tell me about it," he said. "The least the robber barons can do is not afflict the general population with the interest rates some steak-and-potato vice president is getting on his money belt wad."

"They eat pasta salad these days," I said. "And the banks are just trying to tell the public the facts." My defense was only half-hearted; I am—to a larger extent than I've ever told him—my father's son.

"I don't want to know anything banks want me to know," my father said. "It's pollution of the eyes, and the eyes are the portals to the soul. Why cobble up a good soul with dirty money? Do you know what portals means?"

"Yes," I said.

"It's about time," my father said.

The conversation reminded me once again that to my father, the mortal enemy was the Vice President—in whatever form he appeared. I have a feeling that the printed complaint forms you find on the counters of the business are a silent, although misguided, tribute to my father's forty-year war against vice presidents, and something he called "establishment fat."

"When you see the Vice President in his three-piece DuPont suit," my father said to the manager behind the counter at the Stockman's Supply a few years ago when we had come into town to get—among other items—some feed to lure Verbena into the corral, "tell him for me they waste our money wrapping these salt licks in paper that advertises we ought to buy more salt licks. I know how many salt licks I need. Don't cut down trees in Oregon just to be absurd."

The manager, like most store managers who knew my father, stared at the counter and studied the sales slip.

"And don't quote your horse-feed prices for fifty pounds just to make me think it's a bargain when you've raised it ten cents," my father went on. "It's a hundred weight that names the price. Not fifty. Use language to cheat the public, and you'll pay a price you don't know exists. Have you read your Orwell?"

"We had an increase at the home office," the manager said as a last line of defense, forgetting it was best to remain silent in the face of my father's jumping beard.

"Well, don't pass it on to your customers," my father said. "That's madness of the second order."

"We have to," said the manager.

"No you don't," said my father. "Wear out your shoes and grow a garden. It will be good for you. Shoot rabbits in the fall. Tell the Vice President to eat soup and save soap slivers. We do. Take a bath twice a week. If you bathe every day in hot water, your skin will peel off your bones. A little frugality would be healthy for the establishment fat. In the meantime, you can keep your horse feed until the price comes down." That was only one of many times we didn't get around to swimming the pond with Verbena.

Over the years it never occurred to me that we would ever swim Verbena—nor did I understand my father's fascination for insisting we should. The swim seemed the essence of something destined never to be accomplished, a kind of ultimate I'm-a-going to. I do remember, however, when the plan got fixed in my father's mind.

"The internal combustion engine is a bad idea," he said to me one summer afternoon as I was shooting baskets at the goal in our farmyard.

"Yes," I said.

"Don't agree with your father just because he's short," he said.

"OK," I said.

"We're not going anywhere on the farm in the truck anymore," he said. "We're going to use the horse."

"OK," I said. "What about taking trash to the dump?"

"We'll use the truck for the dump," he said.

"What about fishing?" I said.

"We'll use the truck for fishing," he said. My father had a way of compromising immediately. "But we'll use the horse to check the cattle and look at the fences."

"We don't look at fences," I said.

"We're going to start looking at fences," my father said. "On horseback."

"OK," I said.

In order for my father to get onto Verbena, it was necessary for him to use the stump of a cottonwood just outside a shed we called the Electric Company. He would never let me watch him swing into the saddle; instead, he'd dream up some chore for me to do while he led Verbena out of the corral and across the yard. When I'd come back from wherever I'd been sent, there would be my father—full in the saddle—and Verbena would be twisting her head in the air against the bit. Small cyclones of dust would rise around her prancing feet.

"Did you see her buck?" my father said.

"No," I said. "I was in the tool shed. Here's your hoof pick."

"Don't need it now," my father said. "You should have seen her buck. She always bucks when you first get on her. It's what gets your heart started." Then my father would send me off to the north end of the yard to open the gate into the pasture, and out he and Verbena would ride to check fences and peer at our homely steers.

It could all have been done much more quickly in our pickup, but instead, once a week or so, from about the time I was in my early teens until I left for college, my father would ride Verbena through the pastures and back. An hour adventure at most, after which he wouldn't say much—not even during the evening radio news when it was his habit to make a running commentary on the events of the world. But on one such evening, not long before I went to college, my father said:

"Someday I think I'll swim your mother's horse across Big Pond."

"Why?"

"Think what you could learn from that," he said. "Just think."

"What?"

He looked at me over whatever he was reading and shook his head as if he had failed.

"Well," he said. "There's much to learn from swimming a horse—if you contemplate the prospect for awhile."

"What?"

"I don't know yet," he said. "I'm just beginning to think on it. You might do the same. You don't learn anything in this world unless you consider what there is to learn."

"Yes," I said. My father was given to being dismayed at his only son. In fact his only child.

"We'll swim the horse next fall," he said. "When you come back from college for a weekend. It'll fatten up your education. I'm sure it will need it by then." The very next fall my father and I began a rather long tradition of not swimming Verbena across Big Pond.

It was with the knowledge that we would fail to accomplish the swim—a friendly knowledge, now that I think of it—that even after college each fall I'd drive from Kansas City back to the ranch, taking Friday and Monday off to spend the long weekend helping with the various chores that needed doing if we were going to "button up the place" for winter. For three days we'd split and stack stove wood for the Melrose Oak; tack up plastic sheets as storm windows; lower a small evergreen cut from the shelter belt down the chimney to scrape it clean; and lay square bales of straw around the house's foundation against the chance that the great blizzard of '86—my father's favorite historical storm—would reappear. All this, and the great horse swim of Big Pond.

Saturday mornings we would pile into our sturdy Studebaker pickup and, with our coffee mugs spilling onto our jeans and my father's bag of unshelled sunflower seeds dribbling onto the floorboards, prowl the west pastures looking for Verbena—a rather hefty roan of a mare who, as she got older, seemed to feed farther and farther from the house so that our trip to catch her usually covered most of our pastures.

I remember the look she'd give us when we'd pop over some rise and find her browsing peacefully on the late grass coming up in one of the draws that grows wet with the springs that seep out in the autumn. "You guys again," her shaggy visage seemed to say, for even by early October she had grown the remarkable winter wool coat that was her hallmark, and by which my father judged—badly it always seemed to me—the depth and length of the High Plains blizzards he imagined would come roaring down on him out of the Januarys and Februarys in the Dakotas above us.

"Two weeks of snow before the New Year," my father said, rolling down his window and looking at the mare, while his coffee mug steamed a small balloon onto his side of the windshield.

"It didn't turn out that way last year," I said.

"No two years are alike," my father said as a way of putting his past predictions behind him. "You've got to learn to read the coat. Look at that shag; look at how the halter is getting buried in the hair. That's a nasty winter right there on a horse's head."

My father never read a mild weather in Verbena's coat; indeed, some falls he'd want to encircle the house with the huge round bales of prairie hay he had cut off the pastures as winter feed for whatever stock he might be keeping through the winter.

"She always gets a good shag on her," I said. Like cattle trails to our water tank, these conversations were well worn.

"Cold after the first blizzard," my father went on. "Bitter cold. And wind. Blowing snow for a week. I won't be able to see the Electric Company."

"Maybe it won't be that bad," I said.

"Worse," my father said, as he'd point his beard defiantly toward the north. "So bad the television will rattle on about windchill factors and tell me not to go to the horse tank in my boxer shorts."

"They're being helpful," I said.

"Why doesn't the television tell me about Spain if they want to be helpful," he said. "The radio used to tell me about Spain. The *US Farm News* told me about Spain. But no, it took the television two days to tell me Franco was dead. Franco! What a scoundrel! Dead for two days and I didn't know to celebrate."

"Nobody in Western Kansas cares about Franco," I said.

"Well, they ought to," my father said. "You've got to learn something about life besides the price of wheat. Why would the television tell me the wind-chill factor and not tell me that Franco was dead?"

"I don't know," I said. "I don't know." It was my own all-purpose refrain that I'd use—even as a small boy—to change the direction of the conversation, not that I give the technique high marks.

"Do you know what Brendan Behan said about Franco?" my father said.

"No."

About this time Verbena would have edged her way to the truck for the grain we'd put in a bucket in the back. Somehow she knew my father's rant meant food: that, and a harmless walk back to the yard where she'd be fed again, perhaps saddled, but not ridden far, if at all. On balance it must have seemed a good bargain to the old horse. And as chance would have it, she seemed to always stop my father short of telling me what

Brendan Behan had once said about The Generalissimo Franco.

"Catch that horse and put a lead on her before she bolts over the Saline Breaks," my father whooped when, in the middle of his diatribe about Franco and television, he heard Verbena rattling around in the feed bucket in the back of the truck.

"She's not going anywhere," I said.

"She'll be in Nebraska by morning if you don't jump quick." Jumping quick had been my job since boyhood.

What I'd read in the shag of Verbena's head as I snapped a lead to her halter was that the old mare had no intention of bolting through any breaks on her way to Nebraska and into the blizzards lurking in the depth of her coat. It is something a son, at least this son, doesn't tell his father.

"Now you'll learn what there is to swimming a horse," my father said as I got back in the truck. "You'll learn something more than the useful in life. You'll learn something to talk about when you're old and long in the tooth like that horse."

"I expect I will," I said.

"And talk about it at length," he said. "You're too quiet a boy for the good of the country. You've got to learn to scream bloody murder when the four-door Cadillac of capitalism is about to make roadkill of your bony hide."

"I'll speak about it at length," I said. Good, my father would say, and put the truck in gear for the ride back to the yard, Verbena trotting behind.

But no matter how easy it might be to catch Verbena, nor with what efficiency my father and I would get together the tack from various sheds and storerooms, year after year we never got around to swimming her. We'd get close though; some Octobers we'd even get as far as Big Pond itself. And five years ago my father had the idea we should celebrate our impending accomplishment by grilling steaks in a pit fire on the south point that poked itself out into the water.

"Ceremony," I remember my father saying on this occasion, "is a drama we can all write for ourselves." We were cutting cottonwood logs for the fire. Verbena was tethered to a tree, her saddle cinched tight.

"We've got plenty of wood," I said. We had enough for a high school bonfire; my father was as excessive as he was frugal.

"Cut some more," my father said. "I'll want to dry off by the blaze when I come out of that pond, and so will you."

"We've got enough for that," I said.

"Not for both a blaze and a bed of coals for the steaks, we don't," he said. "And then we'll want some fire in the hole to talk by. Don't you want to look across the flames and see your father's face when he tells you what you've learned from swimming a horse?"

"Of course," I said. We cut more wood.

Looking back, I suspect it was all part of my father's dallying dance before the swim. I guess in some dim way I knew that and I was glad for it. Perhaps I sensed we had gotten such a good start on the swim that year I had half a fear we might pull it off. In the end we spent our time in a kind of slow motion puttering: first with the pit, then with the fire; and several times with the horse (my father walked over to Verbena to say something to her and then came away still talking—but to whom I couldn't be sure).

Once, late in the afternoon, he walked around to the dam and along the double line of Russian olives that grew up on each side. I watched him as he looked back at me over the pond. I remember he didn't wave. He stood there a moment. Then he walked back around. As evening came on and the muskrats began to etch their Vs onto the flat water, my father said, "It's gotten away from us again, now hasn't it, son. We've run out of daylight."

"I guess we have," I said.

My father went over to Verbena and unsaddled her and tossed the gear into the pickup.

"I can't teach you about swimming horses in the dark," he said. "It's a lesson of life. You need to see it clearly. You should have been shown long ago." My father looked out over the pond to the other side. "Time flies when you're having fun," he said. "I've never known what to do about that."

"We'll swim her next year," I said.

"For sure," said my father.

We cooked our steaks over the cottonwood coals and talked, the flame dancing in the pit. Verbena didn't go far; as we ate, we could hear her moving through the trees, grazing. Once, I thought I heard her at the pond, taking water.

"Your mother never rode Verbena," my father said as the fire got low.

"I didn't know that," I said. It was getting difficult to see his face. I got up to get another log, but he held out his hand, palm down, to indicate he didn't want me to.

"Your mother wasn't political," he said. In the distance I thought I could hear the night flight of sandhill cranes.

"We'll get it done," my father said.

"OK," I said.

"Her world was flowers," he said.

"You've never told me that."

"We'll swim her horse," my father said.

"Agreed."

But the truth became that, in the years after that evening we cooked our steaks on the pond's bank and listened to the old horse browse among the cottonwoods, we seemed to recede from the swim. The following year we only drove to the pasture and looked at Verbena, while my father held forth on the rising cost of electricity due, he felt (correctly, I suspect), to the new atomic power plant they had installed down the wires from the ranch. A few years later we didn't even get out of the yard, and, had not Verbena come up to the corrals on her own that weekend, I might not have heard my father's dire prediction of yet another bad winter.

"We're not talking the blizzard of '86," he said, as we stood by the horse just before I was to drive back down the highway. "But we are looking at the blizzard of 1912. Or '48. Do you remember the one in '48?"

"I was pretty young," I said.

"Couldn't get out for a month," he said. "You, me, and your mother. All buttoned up in here with rice and beans and pickles. Jerry Simpson would have been proud."

"Call me if you need help," I said.

"Maybe," he said, looking back at the house, "we should have put the round bales around me this year. At least lay them along the north side so I don't get drifted in."

"If you want to," I said. "I've got some time yet. The front-end loader is still on the tractor. It wouldn't take an hour." But he shook his head no, then said:

"You come back next year, and we'll swim that horse first off. Friday afternoon. Make your mother proud of us and teach you something at the same time."

"OK," I said.

"Keep track of what you learn," he said.

"What?"

"Keep track of what you learn from swimming that horse so you can tell me what it is in the long run."

"We haven't done it yet," I said.

"We will," he said. "You've got to get ready by thinking ahead. See the swim in your mind's eye. Watch the water part at her chest. Watch the cottonwood leaves coming down on the pond. Don't think of anything without seeing it in your mind's eye. That's the problem with you vice presidents. You don't watch what you're doing in your head. It's all dry columns and furniture-appliances."

"'Furniture-appliances?" I asked. Generally I don't ask.

"Like dish-washing machines," he said. "God help us."

"I'll try to watch what I'm doing in my head," I told him.

"Good thinking," said my father. "Don't watch television because it will rob you of the ability," he said.

"I know," I said.

As it has turned out, the following year my father swam his horse at last.

My Father, My Mother, and I

We raised each other, my father and I. After we lost Mother, that's what my father used to say when asked about it by some well-meaning relative who wanted to spirit me off to a more normal home. But my father would have none of it: We raised each other like kid goats, he'd say—and we were pleased to do so.

I know it sounds strange because I, too, have watched the television dramas where, with the death of the mother, the father gets older. Or he goes out to find another wife and in so doing becomes serious—or a fool. Sometimes he grows distant with grief and becomes gray to his children, like the back side of a cold front moving east away from you across the pastures. But that's not what happened to my father and me, and it didn't have anything to do with how my father felt about Mother.

Our ranch was small by High Plains standards, so the sign slung under our mailbox announced us as the *Half-Vast Ranch*. My father's self-proclaimed, lifelong case of I'm-going-to was occasionally relieved by fully completed projects. The making of the *Half-Vast* sign was one of them.

"Language is where life is," my father said to me as he burned the H into a cottonwood plank he'd cut from an extra large piece of stove wood. "Get in trouble by what you say," he advised. "That's liberty."

He was a short, muscular man who seemed to be in his body something like the wild burliness of his beard. I took after my mother: thin to gaunt, and taller than my father by the time I was fifteen—as my mother was taller than my father in the pictures of them.

"Liberty," said my father as he burned the wood with a propane torch he'd adapted from a weed burner. "She's a French woman with bare breasts. They won't teach you that in the public school. Bare breasts!"

We had been recently studying "liberty" in civics class (breastless, to be sure) and it was my father's habit to extend my lessons—which he always thought were truncated and Milquetoast at best—into a richer version of political meaning, sometimes illustrated by life as the two of us led it on Half-Vast Ranch, but just as often by wider sources of learning: *Little Blue Books* and the *US Farm News*, both of which gathered like dust bunnies around the house, until once or twice a year—roughly equal to fall and spring cleaning—my father would sort through his piles of "radical paper" and stack it in a small room next to mine in the unheated upstairs of our house. There its continued growth marked my own, but only in height, not (given my father's political sensibilities) in substance.

"What do you know about Bolivia?" my father asked me one winter day after school. I had been feeding Verbena, and my father had taken the chance to browse through my geography book. He was sitting at the kitchen table when I came back in.

"It's where we get our tin," I said.

"And what about South Africa?"

"Gold," I said.

"Madness," my father said. His beard began to twitch as he slowly turned the pages of my textbook. "Every country you study in this book is represented by a picture of either some mineral that is mined by the enslaved population or a crop harvested with the bent backs of the poor."

"I have a test tomorrow," I said.

"You have a test right now," said my father. "Do you know what South African gold and Costa Rican coffee have in common?"

"No," I said.

"They both get shipped to America so the rich can thicken their money belts. Is that what you learn about the countries of the planet?"

"I have to pass the test tomorrow," I said. I had been through this before.

"No you don't," my father said. "What kind of test is this to pass?" Here he waved my book at me. "Tell your teacher Argentina hides Nazi war criminals. Tell him the Negroes in South Africa are slaves. Tell him about the United Fruit Company. Have a hissy-fit. Get hippa-canoris for once in your life. With any luck you'll get in enough trouble they'll call me to school."

I knew better than to get into that much trouble. And I had never gotten *hippa-canoris*—a term my mother had apparently used to describe my father's political rages.

"I have to know what the countries of the world make," I said.

"Oh, really," my father said. His beard twitched. "And what about the countries of the world that don't make anything we use here in capitalist America? I don't see a picture of Tibet in this schoolbook. Did you study Tibet?"

"No," I said.

"How about Goa?" he said. "Did you study Goa?"

"Goa?" I said. At least I had heard of Tibet.

"Goa," he said. "Did you study Goa?"

"No," I said. Not even my world-history professor in college knew much about Goa; how my father developed his interest in it I never learned.

"I thought so," he said. "Goa doesn't sell us anything we can buy and turn into junk, so Goa doesn't exist to the Board of American Education."

By now the point of my father's beard was shaking like a fist. When he'd get angry, the skin on his brow would quiver, and his eyes would widen and narrow as if some hidden camera adjustment were being manipulated to find the light.

"I am the prince of Goa," he bellowed out just as all his facial contortions seemed to come into concert. "I am the prince of Goa, and I take my oath on this text." He rose to his feet holding my geography book in his left hand and slammed the palm of his right hand into the crease of the open pages:

"First, God made idiots," my father recited, as if he were hearing someone saying the words for him to repeat. "That was for practice." Here he paused a moment as if to hear the oath giver. "Then He made school boards." At this point my father peered over my book to see—I suppose—if I were still anywhere in the room, or if I had simply concluded he had gone so hippa-canoris that I had left with the horse for town to get the school nurse. When he reassured himself that his son was still in the kitchen, he said, directly to me: "I am quoting Mark Twain in case someone asks you. Pass on what Mr. Twain has said to your school principal and get in trouble for once in your life. If that doesn't do it, tell your principal you heard Mr. Twain's remarks from the Populist Prince of Goa, a short fat man who happens to be your father. At least get me in trouble. It could be a leg up for yourself."

Although I left for school the next day remembering Mr. Twain's wisdom, much to my father's disappointment I never got into my share of trouble.

❧

"We're going to hang the *Half-Vast Ranch* right under the mailbox and see if the United States Post Office objects," my father said to me the day we made our sign. "See if they stop delivering mail. That's what they did when Cody put his mailbox too high after someone from Hays City blew it down with a shotgun. Oh, where is Sockless Jerry Simpson when we need him? Do you know what *Half-Vast* means?" my father continued.

He had given me the burner so I could burn Vast into the wood. We'd split chores like that: in this case my father had outlined our sign in pencil, fired up the torch and told me to watch as he burned in the first word. Next, I'd get to do my part; then my father would finish, showing me what I had done right and what I had done wrong—only what I had done wrong usually came first, and my father would end his lesson with praise of my efforts, even if that was difficult to do. Sometimes, he'd couple his praise with a small speech about the dignity of work and what a privilege it was to have a nature that enjoyed it. Coming from a man who put off most of life's chores, these talks seemed odd to me, especially as I grew older and began to learn something about the cosmic stresses between body and soul. But then—and even now—what my father had to say about labor never struck me as hypocritical; it was as if he had wanted me to like labor more than he had. Along with getting into trouble, it was his ambition for me.

"*Half-Vast* means we don't have much land," I said. My father looked at me with no little chagrin. I might have been nine or ten at the time, and even though I went to school in Hays and had heard my share of profanity, the pun didn't occur to me. My poor father must have thought me dense; or worse, bland, like "processed cheese" or "even heat"—two virtues of modern life that were being extolled on the radio in those days and against which my father raved repeatedly. It was probably his great fear that he was going to rear a son with neither a sense of outrage nor a sense of humor.

"It's a small joke," my father said grimly, looking at the smoking wood.

"What kind of joke?" I said. I was watching him burn Ranch into the cottonwood slab, and I noticed how his hand shook slightly, how the wood caught fire for a moment when the blue bullet of the flame was on it, and how Ranch came out with a ghost of a wobble to it, as if it wasn't all that sure it had been truly burned into being.

"It's a half-assed joke," my father said as he turned off the propane. "Don't you see?"

"No," I said. At least I was a frank and forthright boy.

"Do you hear me when I say something's half-assed?" my father said.

"Yes," I said. But most every idea I brought home from school in those days was "half-assed." The problem with being a child is that you don't expect your parents—your father in my case—to be more eccentric than your average American historical hero: John Paul Jones, for example who, from my land-locked place on the prairie, seemed pretty wonderful, at least in the placid biographies we were allowed to check out from the school library. But John Paul was never given to railing on about suburban ethics, robber-baron capitalists, the Revised Standard Edition, or "even heat." Not even the vile British got diatribes from John Paul such as my father had dealt out earlier in the week to the local electric company for tacking a surcharge onto our bill:

"See that *sur* in front of charge?" he had said to me. "They want a buck a letter for thinking that up, and a buck more for the hyphen. Committee English always costs the workingman.

Remember that, son. When the Populists come to power, the first thing we'll do is straighten out the language. Speak plain English with a flair, and you can be The Commissioner of Language." By the time I went away to college, my father had offered me a variety of jobs in his future government.

"You think about *Half-Vast* the rest of the day," my father said, as the smoke cleared from our sign. "Use it in a sentence, such as 'a Republican has a half-vast way of thinking.' Try it out in show-and-tell. Instead of bringing a bull snake to class, tell them about some of the half-vast ideas you've found in your geography book."

I knew even then to keep quiet at show-and-tell about my father.

When we finished *Half-Vast Ranch*, we slung it below the mailbox, where it still is today, the wobble in Ranch growing more pronounced over the years.

It is curious, but in many ways our sign's literal meaning turned out to be just as appropriate as its irony. Our ranch was small and not very pretty. The pastures were rocky and filled with soapweed. We didn't have any canyons or breaks. We did have a spot to the northwest of the house where the limestone broke ground and a cut had formed, creating large holes in the bank; there a family of coyotes would raise its young every year. We did, as well, have a shelter belt of locust and cedar that wasn't bad to look at. But for the most part our place was hard-scrabble country.

We did have one thing that was lovely, and we were famous for it: the Big Pond. My father built it himself, and I can remember him doing so—although barely, and in fragments. I remember my mother from this time as well: she seems tall and certain of herself. I recall her at the round waffle iron on Sunday mornings. I see her coming into my room at night to read to me. She is taking me to school and leading me into a room with other children. We walk together down our lane to the mailbox, and she stops coming or going to pick flowers near the end by the road. In all my memories of my mother, I never hear her voice: There are only pictures in my mind, as if in a slow motion silent film.

In the same noiseless way I remember my mother dying— or at least I see in my mind's eye the hospital where I visit her, and days later I see my aunt coming to stay with us. We all move around the house, slowly and in silence.

I see as well the night my father does not come home, and the next afternoon when he does; I see that my mother is dead, although in my memory I cannot make anyone speak to me about it, nor can I see that I understand what it means that my mother is dead.

"Do you remember the summer when I built the pond?" my father would ask me now and again when I was growing up.

"Yes," I'd say. It is not so much a memory as a sense of a memory. Like smoke from a wood stove will stir something in your mind, but you can't be sure what.

When I'd try to recall my father building the pond, it is more through a series of questions about what I see: Am I sitting on the tailgate of the Studebaker, and is my father on a tractor going down the gully that leads to where the dam is forming? Later, do I walk across the crest of that dam and look down at the film of muddy water that is beginning to gather below it? That summer do I notice frogs along the edge? Does my father show me tadpoles in the shallows? During the first winter, do I go down to the pond and see that it is only half full, ice along its edges, with a flock of small ducks huddled in the west slough?

And do I remember for sure the huge, wet snow the spring after my mother died, and how it melted quickly, so that when my father and I went to the pond we discovered it full to the banks, backed up along both sloughs, and edging over the spillway?

"Big Pond," my father claims to have said that day with me standing beside him. "We got ourselves a Big Pond here. I wish your mother could know. She'd feel good about it now."

While our pond grew to be something lovely, over the years our farmyard became a five-acre circle of rusting trucks and tractors and various cobbled equipment in various stages of decay. My father, as it turned out, was given to farm and ranch auctions where he'd buy "iron" with the idea of converting his purchases to some use he imagined we had. The parts we assembled over the years for a log splitter that never got built covered most of the south side of the stone shed: hydraulic hoses, I-beams, two rear axles, and nearly a dozen wheels. And long before energy conservation came into vogue, my father was going to build a wind charger. He even had a plan to sell the excess electricity back to the power company, which, through a regulation my father claimed to have inspired, was obliged to pay us hard cash—or at least reduce our meager bill. To that end, we bought and scavenged assorted rotors and pipes and rusted generators we stacked in a tin shed to the west of the house, the shed that came to be called the Electric Company.

"I was born with the finest case of the I'm-a-Gonnas in Ellis County," my father said to me one day while staring at the rusting iron in the Electric Company. He always seemed amused whenever he contemplated his procrastination, as if he were talking about someone else—someone he was fond of, but someone other than himself.

"I can help," I remember saying, but I remember, as well, my father didn't pay much attention to me.

"Well," he said as he picked up a generator off the pile of junk. "You won't grow old if you postpone everything you're supposed to do, now will you, son?"

"I guess not," I said.

"After I'm dead and gone," he said, "if the Populists come

to power I want you to put me in charge of the Office of Not Getting Things Done. Have them dig up my bones and put them behind a desk with an oak swivel chair. I want to be Commissioner of Procrastination. Do you understand?"

"Yes," I said.

"That's the only way I'll come back from the dead."

"Yes," I said.

One project that did get done—along with the "Half-Vast" sign—was a basketball goal we made for me out of a square of old plywood bolted to a length of oil-field pipe. All through the summers and into the great, long High Plains falls K. C. Jones and Sam Jones of the Boston Celtics—whose team I imagined I was on those days—would sink their long set shots as we defeated again and again a historic all-star team composed of Clyde Lovelette, Dolph Schayes, and George Mikan. I was Bill Russell.

"Good thinking," my father had said when he learned I imagined myself to be a variety of professional basketball players whose exploits we'd hear on the radio at nights. "No sense in staying inside yourself. Get out and pretend to be somebody else. George the Third thought he was a tree. Franco thought he was human. A little madness here and there refines the soul so that it soars above the politics of capitalism. Not that it helped in Franco's case."

"I pretend I'm Bill Russell," I said.

"Do you ever pretend you're anyone else?" he asked.

"No," I said. I was fibbing; going to sleep at night, I'd imagine I was John Paul Jones.

"Too bad," my father said. "Some days I think I'm Sockless Jerry Simpson. I put on my shoes without my socks and give campaign speeches to the mirror in your mother's room." My father's room was always called my mother's room; it was just below mine.

"I don't hear you," I said.

"You're at school," he said. "You wouldn't want to think your father's daft, would you?"

"No," I said.

"Here," he said, and tossed me my basketball. "Go be Bill Russell. How splendid that in America a short fat white man can have a tall skinny black man for a son. There's hope for the damn country yet."

So, amid the junk and the bindweed of our yard, Sam Jones would flick a pass to Bill Russell, who in turn would sink yet another hook shot to win for the Celtics yet another world championship under the dome of the yellow-blue western sky while the Commissioner of Procrastination (alias Sockless Jerry Simpson) looked on with profound approval.

Probably my father thought my imagination held the seeds for a better education than the one I was getting in school. It was not just the school; it was the town itself that bothered him. My father didn't like going to town, as if it tainted him—as if it tainted us. In those days Hays was slowly growing its suburbs into the surrounding pastures.

I remember one fall when I was in high school, the tailgate on the pickup dropped as we sat at a stoplight near Scotty Phillips Hardware. The stove wood we'd cut that morning on the Smoky Hill rolled out onto Eighth Street in front of the station wagons and among the Belle Aires and Impalas that began honking at us—some of which were occupied by the June Allyson look-alike girls who led cheers at my school. When I jumped out to gather up the wood, my father stayed in the truck, rolled down his window, and began to rant at the traffic jam we had caused:

"When the Populists come to power, my son's going to be Commissioner of Vehicles and everybody's going to drive a truck," he bellowed. "Or ride a horse."

My father was not given to yelling in general. His idea was to pick out someone in particular and tell him or even her his story of social injustice; perhaps they'd go tell someone else. It was as if he meant to convert the twentieth-century acquisitive America to nineteenth-century Populism by virtue of gossip, a kind of ripples-on-the-pond theory of political activism. In this particular case he had fixed on my math teacher, a tiny young woman who had just come to Hays from Chicago and who was so startled at the pile of stove wood in the middle of Eighth Street that she had stalled her car and couldn't seem to get it going again. All around her—and us—other cars were honking their horns, and then peeling out to the afternoon football game.

I recall it as one of those fleecy golden afternoons you sometimes get in late October on the plains: so deep with yellow warmth you think it will never grow dark or cold, and if you are a boy in your early teens you can't readily see the point of spending such days cutting wood against the blue-black blizzards of January, much less imagine yourself as the Commissioner of Vehicles.

Neither my math teacher nor I acknowledged one another in the middle of all this honking and ranting; nor did she acknowledge my father—not that it made much difference; he was used to talking to brick walls as well as mirrors. When my teacher finally got her car going again, my father was still in full bellow with a variant of his stock speech about the nature of language and beauty of usefulness.

"Carpets in cars," he yelled at her, "what madness is that? Wait till my boy comes to power. Cars named after African animals and French resorts. What madness is it?"

"That's my teacher," I whispered to my father after I'd loaded the wood and gotten back in the truck.

"What madness is it they bus all the school children to Hays?" he bellowed at the poor woman with renewed vigor.

"*Unification*. What kind of word is that for education? Who wants everybody to learn the same thing? You'll turn our kids into Coke bottles. We'll have to look at their bottoms to see where they come from."

By now she had gotten her car started and was off down the road as fast as prudence would allow. My father continued his monologue for a moment or two, then started the truck and headed up Eighth Street.

"Did you hear me talking?" my father said. "Did you hear what I had to say?"

"Yes," I said.

"What did you learn from all that?" he said; we had begun to weave our way through the streets of Hays out of town toward home.

"I'm not sure," I said.

"Come on," he said. "What did you learn?"

"To check the chain on the tailgate," I said. "And to learn from my mistakes." To learn from one's mistakes had been that week's theme in civics class.

"That's not what you learned," my father said. "You can always pick up wood. Labor is never a waste. If the only learning you acquire is from your mistakes, you'll grow up to be a capitalist and live in a place like that." Here my father pointed to a two-story imitation English Tudor house that was getting built on a treeless lot near the golf course on the edge of Hays. "With matching furniture," he went on. "Carpet over good wood floors so you can't hear the creak of yourself walking. And air-conditioning to steal your summers. Do you want that for a life? Do you want never to be hot or cold, and to live in a house with no sounds of its own except little electric motors running all the time? Is that what you want?"

"I wish my clothes didn't smell like wood smoke," I said.

"What?" my father said.

"I heard some kids talking about me the other day," I said. "They made fun of me because I stink like wood smoke."

"What do they smell like?" my father asked.

"They don't smell," I said. "Maybe the girls smell of perfume sometimes," I said.

"Dried and boiled French flowers," said my father, more to himself than to me. Then he was quiet for a moment; his beard was still. I think now he must have been considering whether to have one of those heart-to-heart talks fathers and sons have—usually over sex, of course, but in this case it would have been over the differences between the poor and the rich, the country and the town, us and them. He might even have thought to go on at some sympathetic length about the virtues of our life in an effort to console his son. But to my father's credit, he resisted the temptation; he was the same man to me as he was to my mother's mirror: "If you don't smell of your own life, you're the living dead," he said. "Which would you rather be? The living dead or stink of cottonwood smoke?"

"I'd rather stink," I said. I wasn't sure that was true, and no doubt my hesitation was reflected in my voice, but my father didn't take me up on it.

"Well," he said, "that's one thing you learned today. Now think about the rest of what you learned and tell me about it at great length sometime."

"Yes," I said.

"At great length and full of details, as if your mother were listening and needed to catch up," he said.

"I will," I said.

On the road home I remember seeing a long line of snow geese in a ragged V heading south.

"Early blizzards," said my father as he looked at them through the windshield. "We'll check Verbena's coat to see how bad it will be." He grinned through his beard. It was his deep

grin: to be free from Hays was added to the thought of tough-
ing it out through a big winter at the ranch. Round hay bales in
circles against the blizzard of '86.

"Your mother loved snow at night," he said as we bolted the
Studebaker over Seven Hills Road on the way to the Half-Vast
Ranch. "She would get up in the dark and stand at the window
and watch the yard fill up. You were born in a snow. Whenever
it snowed your mother would say it was you drifting through
the universe." These words of my mother's were the only ones
I ever heard my father speak.

The Commissioner of Procrastination: 1904-1987

"To swim a horse across water," my father said to me, "you do
not take off the saddle. Water doesn't hurt the saddle. You'll
need to neatsfoot oil it of course, but water itself doesn't hurt
leather." I nodded.

It was Friday afternoon; I had come home as promised, es-
caping—my father pointed out in the first minutes after my ar-
rival—the impending crash of various financial markets, which,
in his opinion, damn well deserved to tumble down on top of
me if I insisted in living off the backs of the working poor.
We were sitting at the kitchen table. Outside, it was a warm
gold-and-blue day. Windless. When I was a boy, it had been my
job to neatsfoot oil all the leather we had between us: boots,
saddles, an old rifle scabbard my father had bought at farm auction against the day he was going to get a rifle to shoot a deer.

"OK," I said. "Let's put oil leather on the weekend list. I'll
do that."

"Good thinking," said my father. He seemed dreamy, as if
there were something he was trying to recall but couldn't. He
fiddled with his beard; over the years it had grown two tufts to
it, a kind of forked beard; and while it had gone gray, it had not

turned white: My father looked in old age like some wizened satyr, modestly pleased with himself, but a little lost.

"First off," he continued rather abruptly after a moment of silence and with no prompting from me, "you ride your horse directly into the water; don't let him turn away from the swim at hand." I realized my father always called horses "he" or "him," no matter what their sex; in this case Verbena had been a mare for over thirty years.

"Yes," I said.

Usually my father took the Friday afternoon of my visit to bring me up to date on the state of politics in the country: a kind of who's who of the nation's leading rascals. After that, we'd make up a list of chores that needed doing, and often we'd get a start on them before evening. Later, at dinner, it had become our custom to lay out once more the horse-swimming plans, but until this particular weekend that had never included any real instruction on how the swim was to be made.

"When you get your horse out into the water where he can swim by himself," my father said, now more calmly, "you slide off to the left and hold on to the saddle horn with your right hand. Do you understand?"

"Yes," I said.

"Don't fight the water," said my father. "A horse will tow you along peacefully if you don't thrash about and if you let your feet come up, which they will, boots and all."

"OK," I said.

"Notice you can swim a horse without being able to swim yourself," my father said, "and cross a river or a pond in spite of your deficiency." Both my father and I could swim.

"I understand," I said.

"Now when you get to the other side of the pond," my father continued, "let your horse find his feet, and then come out beside him, walking yourself. Don't get lazy and think you'll keep your boots from getting muddy by slipping into the saddle at the last minute and riding your horse out. Let him come out by himself. Stand back and he'll shake."

"Yes," I said.

My father grew quiet: He had that distant look in his eyes. A hackberry tree had grown up over the house and its branches were beginning to touch the tin roof. When a breeze came along you could hear the tree scrape, as it did while my father and I sat at the table for a moment in silence.

"You want me to cut that tree back this weekend?" I said.

"No," he said. He seemed to have lost track of himself.

"You want to get started on the chores yet this afternoon?" I said. "We can put some square bales around the base of the house." He shook his head no, then:

"Why don't you shoot some baskets?" There hadn't been a basketball around the place in years.

"We got work to do," I said. "If you're going to make it through winter."

"We'll make it through the winter tomorrow," he said.

"OK," I said.

"You know why I'm short?" he said.

"No," I said.

"To live a long time," he said. "You don't see very many tall old men, now do you?" he said.

"No, I don't," I said. He pulled at the left fork of his beard.

"The Big Pond was the last project I saw through to the end," he said.

"There were others," I said.

"Not many," he said.

"It wasn't the point," I said.

"Shoot some baskets," he said. "Pretend you're Bill Russell. I want to read some radical paper. We'll eat turkey legs and rice at six."

"I'll cook," I said. "I've brought some things from town."
I'd picked up a roast and some potatoes.

"Pizza?" he said.

"What?"

"You didn't bring pizza?" he said. "I won't have it on the
place. Imagine what it does to your colon. I want turkey legs
and rice. They're in the ice box."

"OK," I said.

"I'm going to read," he said. He got up and went into
Mother's room.

I spent the afternoon laying square bales around the foundation of the house. Some years, when my father was convinced
there would be a great snow, we'd use the John Deer to circle
the whole yard with the large round bales of prairie hay he'd
cut off the flat of our pastures.

Once I went out to the basketball goal and looked at it. The
net was gone, and the rim was rusted. But the Boston Garden
looked much the same, even though some bindweed was creep-
ing in on the western edge of the parquet. I took an imaginary
shot and made it.

Around sundown I came back to the house. I could smell
the cottonwood smoke in the yard and knew that my father had
fired up the Melrose oak to boil his turkey legs. We had a fine
dinner at the kitchen table and spent the evening talking about
the time we'd lost the load of wood on Eighth Street. I was going to tell my father some of what I'd learned that day, but he
put his finger to his lips and shook his head.

"Keep it in," he said, as his finger bouncing against the shag
of his beard and mustache that in winter he'd let close in over his
mouth. "Keep it in until it grows wings and talons and flies out of
you by itself. It will soar. It will find me. It will have good eyes."

The next morning when I got up, my father was out of the
house. I poured myself some coffee and read *The Farm News*:

The editorial letters were about the Middle East and parity. The quotations at the bottoms of the columns ran from Gandhi to Reagan. I thought my father might have gone to town.

"I've got Verbena," he said, as he came in a few minutes later.

"I could have helped," I said.

"It wasn't any trouble," he said. "I talked to her about Franco and she came right over."

"Do you want to swim her today?" I said.

"Was Jerry Simpson sockless?" my father said.

"Let's line out some chores first," I said.

"Let's not and say we did," said my father. The twin points of his beard were shaking with an excitement I had not seen in him before.

"OK," I said.

We went outside. Verbena was saddled and tied to the chain latch on the bed of the pickup.

"You drive ahead," said my father. "The horse and I will come along."

"You sure you don't want to wait until it warms up?" I said. "Later this afternoon." It was a bluebird day but cool. It was never clear to me who was going to swim this horse. Speaking for myself, I wanted a little warmth when I came out of the Big Pond.

"Get going," he said. "Do as your father says or I won't let you in my government when the revolution comes." He untied the horse.

I got in the truck and drove it down to the pond. As I left the yard, I checked the mirror and saw my father heading for the cottonwood stump by the Electric Company. When I got to the Big Pond, there were teal in the west slough, and they took off and circled once and then went over the hill. I drove to the dam and got out and lowered the tailgate and sat on it. Pretty soon I could see my father coming over the hill on Verbena; against the brown of buffalo grass pasture he looked like something from a poster you'd find in a western art gallery.

"How is she?" I said when they got to the truck. I noticed that in recent years Verbena had been growing a gathering of her random white hairs into a small cluster in the middle of her forehead.

"Old," my father said. "But full of piss and vinegar."

"She's as old as I am," I said. "Older than you if you count horse years."

"You should have seen her buck when I got on," my father said.

"You want me to swim her?" I said. I thought that might be best.

"What do you know about swimming a horse?" my father said.

"You just taught me," I said. "Last night up in the kitchen."

"That was talk," he said.

"You ever swim a horse?" I said.

"No," he said. He reined Verbena around in a circle. "Don't ask me questions you know the answer to. What madness is that?"

"Well," I said, "we're about even when it comes to swimming horses."

"No, we're not," my father said. On the point of land across the way a breeze came up and sent a shower of cottonwood leaves over the pond. We both watched them as they settled on the water.

"You're right," I said. "It's time you swam your horse."

It is two days later: Monday, and I am getting ready to go back to Kansas City. My father and I are standing in the front yard of the house. It is circled by the large, round hay bales he has convinced me to tractor up in advance of an impending blizzard.

"You wait and see," he says.

"For what?" I say.

"The yard will be full to the round bales with snow and the television will babble on about the frozen dead out here."

"It won't be that bad," I say.

"Worse," he says.

"I think you'll make it," I say.

"Maybe," he says. He doesn't say anything for a moment, then: "I'm not going to watch television anymore."

"OK" I say.

"You don't sell waterbeds, do you?" he says.

"Mortgage insurance," I say. "Why?"

"They're selling waterbeds on television," he says. "Chairs that vibrate. Plastic doohickeys that shoot sliced cucumbers into salads."

"What madness is it?" I say.

"It's 1886 and I am Sockless Jerry Simpson," he says, looking up through the circle of hay bales at the round blue above us. "The frozen night is coming up my legs, but I am looking for an eagle who is looking for me."

"What?" I say. I look at him to see if he is all right.

"At least I don't have to ride around this country trying to find out where I am," he says. "I get to stay put. Historical cold. You will be the snow in the universe."

I don't know what to say, and we stand together in silence.

That Saturday my father swam her here, he told me to walk around to the point on the other side of the pond and watch him from there.

"You can't learn about swimming a horse without watching me do it head on," he said.

When I got to where I could see my father, he had dismounted and was patting Verbena on her rump. A small cloud of dust came off and floated away in the slight breeze. Then he ground tied her and walked along the water's edge toward the dam. I couldn't tell what he was doing. The horse looked after him. In a moment he came back, and I wondered how he would get into the saddle without his tree stump, but he seemed to spring onto Verbena, jumping his foot into the backward-facing stirrup and swinging himself into the saddle in a sure manner like a western-movie cowboy.

Verbena was startled for a moment, then did a little crow-hop buck. My father made a circle to the left and came straight at me into the pond. Verbena kept her head up and her nostrils were flared.

"Answer a letter with a letter," my father finally says as we stand in the yard amid the round bales. "Not with a phone call. Don't put money in Ma Bell's pocket. Don't call me on Father's Day or New Year's or Easter. Don't send me any of those stupid greeting cards. Greeting Card. What kind of language is that? It's nothing but a gimmick so the Vice President can slip his hand into your pocket while you're under the spell of the great blue hump of sentimentality. If they don't get rich on the raw red backs of the working poor, they do it on the sentimentality of the middle class."

"I understand," I say.

"Do you read what I mail you?" he asks. "Have you read your Veblin? Have you read the Little Blue Books? I don't want to be sending this stuff into the void. The post office doesn't censor mail anymore. Thank God we won that battle."

"We did," I say.

"Don't eat Velveeta cheese," my father says. "Or Ann Page bread."

"I won't," I say.

"Not even rats will eat white bread," he says. "That's why they made it in the first place, so mice and rats wouldn't shit in the flour."

"I think you're right," I say.

We shake hands and stand there in the circle of huge hay bales and look at the ridge they make around the house. Toward the east, I can see the top of my basketball goal.

"Did you notice that white patch that's coming out on Verbena's head?" my father says after a moment.

"I told you I did," I say. He nods.

"Historical cold," my father says.

"It's a tough winter in the shag of the horse," I say.

"You're beginning to learn," he says.

"I guess I am," I say.

From where I was on the point, I could see that once Verbena started swimming my father slid off her left side. The reins were draped over her neck, and with his right hand he held onto the saddle horn. But his feet hadn't come up, and he was slipping through the water at an angle. There was a slight wake at his neck, and it was breaking into his beard. He seemed to be looking at some point just in front of himself.

"How you doing?" I shouted. He didn't answer. It was a long swim. It was the longest line you could take across Big Pond. Near the middle, Verbena turned her head south to look down the slough and then back north again toward the dam, so there was a little S to her wake at that point. By then the ripples of their swim were beginning to reach the pond's edges, and the cottonwood leaves and small branches that had been floating on the water were bobbing slightly.

"How's it going?" I yelled. Again my father didn't answer. They kept coming at me. The teal I'd jumped earlier crested the ridge to the east of the pond and circled us once then hustled back over the hill. Some wind sent another small storm of leaves adrift in the air, and they sailed out over the pond, Verbena, and my father.

"You OK?" I said again. No answer, only firm swimming straight ahead.

When my father found his feet at the pond's edge and stood up in the mud of the shallows with some wet leaves clinging to him and with water running out of the cuffs of his shirt and dripping from his beard he said:

"It didn't get away from us this time, now did it son?"

"No," I said. "It didn't." Verbena shook and the spray of water made a rainbow around her.

"Did you know your mother named this horse?" said my father, still standing with Verbena in the water and brushing off the leaves from his shirt.

"I didn't know that," I said.

"She named this horse for that batch of flowers we got at the end of the lane," my father said.

"I know those flowers," I said.

"So do I," my father said. "I'd pick some for your mother now and then to make up for my madness."

"Do you need help?" I said.

"Who knows?" he said.

In a moment, he seemed to gather himself and walked out through the mud and up onto the bank. The horse shook again, and my father stomped his boots and water shot out of the seams at the soles.

"How was it?" I said.

"Your mother would have been proud of us," he said. "That's her in the head of the horse. The white coming out. That's your mother."

"Yes," I said.

"I wonder where I'll wind up," he said. "I want to be a soaring bird. Some great soaring bird with eyes so good he can spot the wobble in Ranch on the Half-Vast sign. Did you ever notice that?"

"Yes," I said.

I tried to get my father to let me lead Verbena back to the house, but he wouldn't hear of it.

"Give me a boot lift into the saddle, son," he said. "It's about time I let you do something for me."

I followed them in the truck. The sun was to the south and warm; it was the kind of warmth that cuts through the coolness, and it warmed each one of us, and we in turn warmed the surrounding air. When we got to the house, my father gave me Verbena and went inside to change his clothes.

That afternoon we started doing the chores we usually did to get him ready for winter, and that evening I brought the saddle and other gear in by the Melrose and gave them a good coat of neatsfoot oil while we talked. My father seemed subdued.

"What did you learn from swimming a horse?" he said at last.

"That it can be done," I said. After all these years I thought I'd try a little irony on my poor father. It didn't work.

"That's not all there was to learn," he said. There wasn't any rancor in his voice; his beard did not shake itself at me.

"How about you?" I said. "What did you learn?"

"I'd rather not say," he said. Perhaps it was the flat way he spoke that made something like Verbena's shake when she came out of the pond go through my body. My father noticed it, and his eyes widened for a moment.

"You OK?" he said.

"Yes," I said. We listened to the tree scrape the roof. I felt as if I had come through some historical place and was on the other side: There the light was lively and open, bright as a High Plains summer morning. I could hear my father talking; he was speaking out of the light, and what he had to say was not in words but in the chunks and particles of our life: boots and generators and language and hoops and straw and trucks and wood and sorry cattle. And me. Standing in the stream of lovely rubble, I saw my mother.

"Do you remember your mother?" my father said.

"I don't remember the sound of her voice," I said.

"Neither do I," said my father. He looked at me as if to test his memory of who I was.

"Tell me about mortgage insurance," he said.

"You don't want to know," I said.

"You don't cheat the working poor, do you?" he said.

"No," I said.

"You don't think time's money, do you?"

"No."

"Do you know what gossamer means?" he said.

"Yes."

"There's some hope in the world yet," he said.

"I may not be it," I said.

"You might be," he said. "I was."

That was Saturday night. We worked together two more days to button up: plastic storm windows, stove black, wood, square bales, round bales.

On Monday before I leave we are standing together in the yard.

"The blizzard of 1886," says my father.

"I think you're right this time," I say.

"Keep me in mind," he says. He taps his head, then lays his hand on mine. I realize we have not touched each other much over the years. "See your father in your mind's eye," he says.

"I can't do anything else," I say.

"Good thinking," he says.

The winter was mild, but in the spring two back-to-back blizzards buried the ranch, and my father was stuck for weeks. The phones were dead. The power lines were down. I drove out.

When the neighbors and I got into the yard by using a tractor to clear the lane, we found him in the yard amid the round bales sitting on Verbena in the snowy sunshine.

"I would have made it out by myself," he said to me as I came through the drifts. "But I didn't know why I should. This horse and I have been riding in circles once a day and talking to keep in practice."

"Keep in practice for what?" I said.

"Somebody's got to stay honest," he said.

After everyone left and I was alone with him, he told me he'd heard my mother's voice during the second blizzard.

"It's a delicate voice," he said. "With small blue petals in it. She asked about you."

"Yes," I said.

Words Make a Life

He Could Fix Anything

My father was tall, taller than I am. He grew old gracefully, my mother would say. He had red hair that stayed red until his fifties, then went only slightly gray. His hands were large, but his fingers were long and delicate. He might have been a pianist. When he smiled (which was seldom, but not because he was an unhappy man), you had a sense he was enjoying himself immensely, and in ways he chose not to explain. "Nothing, my dear," is what he would say to my sister when she'd ask. "Nothing at all."

"He's pleased to have fixed something at the garage," my mother would say.

At work he wore blue bib overalls (that had a plethora of pockets), no cap, and steel-toed work boots. In the left-hand breast pocket of his overalls, he kept his pens and chalk markers, two tire gauges, and a pencil magnet.

He was a neat man who, when not bending over an engine, stood straight and walked straight. His tools were cleaned and his workbench set in order each night. The floor was swept, and the nuts and bolts and washers and cotter pins that had fallen onto it were put into a bucket and sorted into coffee cans on Saturdays between pumping gas.

There was a shower in the garage that he would use before

he walked home in clothes he kept clean for supper. At home his fingernails were never dirty. In the mornings, he would walk back to work in the same clothes, put them on hangers and change. On Saturdays, he would bring home his overalls, and my mother would wash them on Sunday along with his "travel outfit."

When explaining a car's problem to a customer—whether it was the engine or the brakes or the transmission or the cooling system—my father would spread his arms full length if the matter was serious, less so if it was not, and hold his hands apart in front of him if the solution was simple. Changing a tire that was out of round to correct a front-end wobble was simple. A new front-end suspension required the full width of my father's rather long arms. As he explained what needed to be done and how he would do it, my father would bring his hands together, (sometimes pausing for a detailed digression about where he was going to get the tie rods and why he might not need to change both of them) until his hands met at a clap of the job completed. He would smile. He could fix anything.

When he died the bucket had been sorted.

Our Mother

"You'll need a dictionary," my mother said before I went to college. "Pick three words a day, even if you think you know them. But not in ABC order. That way you won't get bored. Open the dictionary, find a word, learn it, then write it on a slip of paper. Like a bookmark. Do you know what domain means? You need to make up for the words you missed. Plethora?"

She was referring to a grade school year when I was a sickly child with a case of acute tonsillitis that resulted in earaches, high fevers, and many days absent from class.

"Words make a life," she'd say while washing the evening's dishes. "Do you know what countenance means? Atonement?"

A Short History of Blanks

I design books: *Gutters* and *case backs*, *rivers* and *verso*, *quarto*, and *signature* are the nomenclature of my trade. Or were when I started. *Format* and *galley proof*. I understand I am un-hip, as if I were to use *Hi-Fi* instead of *stereo*—which I do. *Mono*, I am told by Lillian, my sister's late-in-life daughter, is a disease. It used to be music as well: the kind that came from the lid of a forty-five record player: "Memories Are Made of This."

At first I worked at Hallmark here in Kansas City. Now I freelance. My Plaza apartment is my office. The Country Club Plaza, Kansas City, Missouri. Mr. and Mrs. Bridge's domain. Calvin Trillin slurping a frosty at Winstead's.

Over the years I have spread into many rooms: computers and scanners and light tables throughout. Tastefully throughout.

At Hallmark I designed "favorites": 20 Favorite Sonnets by Shakespeare. 100 Favorite Love Poems. 50 Favorite Words of Wisdom. 100 Famous Quotations by American Women. I also designed "paths": 50 Paths to Wisdom. 25 Paths to Bliss. No one ever suggested 50 Ways to Leave Your Lover.

I was not cynical about such work then, nor am I now. If my book buyers want their wisdom "famous" and flush left in purse-sized octavos, who am I to judge? We all have our paths.

These days I design address books. I design recording calendars, sometimes called *agendas*. I do not design memoirs (fictional or not). I design exhibition catalogues: *A Painter's Room of One's Own*. I design coffee table books: *Joyce's Paris. Small Hotels of Italy. A Place in the World Called Seville*. And once, a small duodecimo for autographs.

Among my favorite projects have been two Abecedarians. One was for painting: *M is for Matisse* (with a lovely black-haired young woman in an afternoon pose). A second was for writers whose pictures appeared like a watermark behind their letters with their text at the bottom C: "It was said that a new person had appeared on the sea front: a lady with a little dog."

I also design *blanks*—books with empty pages for memoirs to be written or diaries to be kept. Or not. I am Mr. Tabula Rasa of Kansas City. And many other cities as well.

I like what I do. There is a pleasing philistine sensibility about a well-designed, large-format book that features the flora and fauna from the French impressionist period. The philistine sensibility is not in the book but in the plush homes and apartments where Monet's "Water Lilies" or Fantin LaTour's "Still Lives" languish. I test my designs against the horizontal of coffee tables, not the vertical of bookshelves.

"Did you do this?" My sister asked me when she and Gerhard had me for dinner not long ago. I specify that the publishers not include my name in the credits.

She showed me a coffee-table book that featured paintings of women in New York museums: "Madame X" from the Metropolitan, a Vermeer from the Frick. Picasso's "Two Nudes" from MOMA. Others. I had been inspired by an old *Playboy* photo series: The Women of Rome (they were riding topless on Vespas); The Women of San Francisco (they were hanging out of both their blouses and the cable cars on which they rode).

"Not that you always fess up," she said.

"It's one of mine," I said. "Fess up" is what our mother used to say when trying to find out who spilled orange juice on the kitchen counter.

"Lovely," she said. I keep it out.

My sister's diary, an early blank of mine (a garden motif with flowers) also in the living room that night was (I took a peek) blank: Hours without alphabets. Days without words. Impatience without patience. It was sitting next to a book of mine on the gardens in Tuscany, but since Elaine did not ask about either, I said nothing.

On whatever coffee table I am, I want to be featured, even if anonymously. My aim is to be number one on the bestseller lists of unread, stacked books in the magazine homes of America. *The Gardens of Tuscany* in an agreeable arrangement with *The Women in New York's Museums*.

The Text of Spark Plugs

The week before I left for college, I took my second-hand Ford to the garage so we could change the oil and rotate the tires. My father was there even though it was past closing. Sometimes he would work until my mother called him to come home or sent me to get him; other times he would go back to work after supper. In summer, when he came home late, he'd get himself a beer and sit in a webbed lawn chair beside a pedestal-mounted blue glass globe. We could hear him talking to himself into the evening. Once, returning from the pool where I was a lifeguard, I sat with him.

"You're a strange kid," he said to me.

I didn't know what to say.

"Your mother likes you," he said after a moment.

I thought this was my father's way of saying he liked me, too.

"I've got a new set of plugs," my father said from above the car while I was in the pit draining the oil.

I could tell by the sound of his socket wrench that he was taking my old ones out. Not that I had asked him to, although they needed changing.

"Thank you," I said.

"New wires too," he said.

"I can do that," I said.

"Points."

"Sure. Thanks."

"Dwell."

"Not necessary. But thank you. I can help you with the Studebaker before I go," I said.

"When you come back," he said.

Then there was the quiet you get among mechanics. The sigh of a stubborn bolt coming free. The small thud when a nut hits the floor. The roll of a washer like a coin. Closed-lipped grunts and groans that formed a patois—not that I knew that word then, nor was it among my mother's words. Finally, my father, again, from above:

"Don't disappoint your mother."

"I'll try not to. I have my dictionary."

"I mean with women."

"Yes."

"Do you know about women?"

"Some."

"I didn't think so."

"What should I know?"

By now the oil had been drained, and I had put on a new filter. I climbed out of the pit and found the oil cans and a metal spout. The car took five quarts if you replaced the filter. When I finished filling the crankcase, I stood by the fender. My father was bent over the engine putting the spark plug wires in place.

"What should I know?" I asked again. "About women."

"If they break you can't fix them like cars," he said. He replaced the distributor cap, and wiped his hand with his shop rag.

"I see," I said.

"But then we can't be fixed either," he said.

He put out his hand, and I shook it. I noticed more than a

small tremor among his fingers and something odd about his eyes as he looked at me.

It was my mother who told me years later, after he had died, that my father once loved another woman. It was my sister Elaine who told me that our mother had once loved another man.

"But it was before they were married," she said, as we were driving back from visiting their graves.

"For them both?"

"I don't think so. But they knew. They must have told each other."

"Atonement," I said.

"Yes."

Dinah Shore

When my sister was young she looked like Dinah Shore. She could enter a room with the same television-show skirt flourish, which she would make to the amusement of those who understood her parody, our father among them. And like Dinah, my sister could sing silky torch songs: "A Small Hotel," "Dancing on the Ceiling," "The Way You Look Tonight."

These days she has about her a Joanne Woodward countenance. She said she was hoping for a Grace Kelly face as she aged (modesty is not one of her virtues). I think Joanne Woodward suits her better. Recently she has reverted to Dinah, singing "My Funny Valentine."

"Are you thinking of someone?" I asked her.

"Yes."

"Do I know him?"

"No."

Like me, she is tall, at least taller than our mother, but not as tall as our father. Unlike the matrons of her society, she is lithe.

I think a man other than her husband would find her winsome as she is. I wonder if she has lovers—or has had lovers. Should a brother ask?

She wears little makeup, has auburn hair with touches of gray, stands straight, and walks with ease; bright, alert, I have seen her suppress a smile at something up ahead during one of our walks through a nearby park: a lady with a dog pulling her toward a wing-clipped goose. Always when we see old men sleeping on benches.

Once, when a man I didn't know passed us on a sidewalk.

Talking

After I graduated from college, and after my father had died, I lived with my mother for a summer, while lifeguarding at the local pool as I looked for full-time work.

One evening when I came home, she was sitting in the front lawn by my father's globe. Both chairs were out. I sat in my father's chair.

"I talk to him," my mother said.

The evening was summer in that fullness that says there is no other season. We were quiet for a moment.

"He talked to himself," I said.

"He said he talked to you before you went to college. Something about women."

"Yes."

Again: quiet.

"Did Elaine have to…?"

"Yes."

This time the silence between us was longer.

"I'm not going to tell him," my mother said.

"Did you ever tell mother I was pregnant before…?"

"She knew."

The Studebaker

It was a maroon convertible. Two door. There was a joke in those days that you could not tell if a Studebaker was going forward or backward because the front and the rear were streamlined.

My mother and I were alone in my father's garage. The Studebaker was there, parked as if ready to go.

"We had to sell it to get you out of the hospital," my mother said. "We came home from the University Medical Center with you on the bus. Your father walked to the garage until he made a deal with Bob Snow on a car. But that was for me to drive. He never gave up walking to work. He said it was good practice for poverty. I never told him about the money."

"What money?"

"Your uncle Conroy sent me money. He was a doctor by then."

"To pay the medical bills?"

"For a car."

"The Studebaker?"

"No. The Studebaker was gone. We'd see it driving around with the top down, and I got so I couldn't look when it passed by. Your father courted me in that car. He was so pleased when he bought it back and you two restored it. But…"

My mother seemed to have lost track of what she was going to say. She went over to my father's workbench and looked at his tools, touching some of them. We had sold the garage and everything in it to pay for his medical bills; the Studebaker (for a second time, I had just learned) included. My mother got a work rag and dusted the hood.

"What car did you buy with Uncle Conroy's money?" I asked.

"Your Ford."

"I thought that was a trade. Something about work father was doing for the used-car dealer in town."

"It wasn't enough," she said. "I put in a hundred from Conroy. And when your father bought back the Studebaker as well. Only then it was money I'd saved."

"Did he…"

"Both times he thought he'd gotten a good deal. Why not let a man think that? Good deals are important to men."

"It runs," I said.

Its top was up. I unhooked the latches and pulled it back. I opened the passenger door. I turned the key, but not so far as to crank the engine. Ignition lights came on. I pumped the break.

"I don't want to," my mother said.

"You sure? I can take you for a drive."

"I've been sitting in it now and then. I'd rather leave it at that," she said. "But keep the top down."

A Portrait of Our Mother

She had gray hair from as long as I can remember, a wide forehead and pale blue eyes. Her arms were short, and in contrast to my father, she walked with a slight—a very slight—stoop, more a bending forward as if to get where she was going by putting her head in that direction.

A traveling one-armed painter my father hired one year did a portrait of her as her Christmas present.

The woman in the painting seems a little sad. At least sadder than when we were growing up, but not as sad as after my father died. I can think of no portrait of a woman from any period of art history that resembles it. The one-armed painter got the eyes right, the forehead, and hair. If she could speak out of it, she would say: *The quintessential me. More for the word than for the fact.*

"May I have it?" My sister asked as we were cleaning out the house.

"Yes."

"When did you realize it was mother?" she asked.

"Not long ago. And you?"

"Not until now."

My Turn

By the time my father and I had finished refurbishing the Studebaker, he was too weak to drive. Once after lifeguarding, I stopped by the garage, parked the Ford, and took the Studebaker the rest of the way home, honking as I came up to the house. My father was sitting by his globe. My mother came out of the kitchen, wiping her hands in a dishtowel. We helped my father get in front, and she got in back. I drove up and down the streets of our neighborhood, past the garage, then across the street into my high school's parking lot.

"My turn," my father said.

I got out and helped him around to the driver's side. My mother joined him in front. The top was down. Off they went. My mother waved her hand in the air.

I walked to the garage and drove my car home. When I got there the Studebaker was in the driveway, but my father's chair was bereft.

The One-Man Woodcutter

Clayton made me promise I'd tell his story. This is it. He's dead.
That's part of the story. How he died and all. Cutting wood.
This big rotten tree limb that broke out and killed him down
on the Whitewoman. How I found him. Why he was called the
One-Man Woodcutter. I'm the widow.

Not that I want to tell about it. But he made me promise.
He was always making me promise something. Don't give more
than a dollar at church. Promise to fix me bierocks for supper
on Saturday. Don't tell those women in Cottonwood anything
about us. Not your sister about Casey. Nobody about Casey.
Promise now! Casey's our daughter. She's dead too.

They're always telling you what to do. That's all a promise
is. Just telling you what to do. I don't much like it. When he
was dying, he'd come to now and then and have me promise
something else. Change the oil every three thousand miles. Put
the screen over the flue pipe in the spring. Give the welding tools
to Tony. He loaded me with a pickup full of promises. I think
he died before we got him to the hospital, but they never told
me one way or the other. When I finish his story, I'll do things
my way.

We live in Whitewoman County. In Bly. Not that anybody'd
know about Bly. There's not much left. Tony works on the Cody
ranch between here and Blaze. He's a hermit. Lives in a hut on

Big Oxbow just off the river. They call him Flatshot. He's our son. Casey's buried in Denver. That was years ago. Why she's buried in Denver and not here in Bly. I must have promised him that fifty times. Maybe I'll tell. Maybe I won't. I'm thinking about it. I'd like to be rid of it, I can tell you that much.

What Clayton did before he cut wood was weld. He had his shed on the highway north of Bly with his tools and torches and iron in it. He'd go there every day but Sundays and be home around dark, filthy to the bone. Before he'd come inside, I'd have him bathe in the canning house where he'd rigged a shower because I made him. You can't have them in your clean house all nasty and shedding dirt like they're a dog in summer. I don't let Levi in whatever the time of year, why should I let in a dirty man? Levi's the dog. He sleeps outside in the back of Clayton's truck. Even now, he's there.

When Clayton got the first layer off, he could come in. I had this robe in the canning house for him. And slippers. I had things arranged. Then he'd shower inside a second time. On Saturdays he'd give me his work clothes to wash. They'd be so full of grime and burn holes and dirt I'd put them in the Kenmore by themselves. Then I'd run it through once empty to wash the tub out. At least everything would be clean for Jesus on Sunday. Not that Clayton went to church or had much to do with Jesus. My sister Ellen and I are Lutherans. Missouri Synod Lutherans. Clayton made me promise not to bury him in the church cemetery but out of town in the country cemetery with the pagans.

"You think Clayton will be going with us to the service Sunday?" Ellen says.

She knows better because her Albert didn't go to the service either. Ellen and I talk back and forth here in Bly, feeding our birds.

"You think Albert will be popping out of the ground for

dinner?" I say back. It's not as mean to say as it sounds.

"If Clayton goes to service, Albert will be to dinner," my sister says.

How Clayton got so filthy every day was that welding shed of his. It had this dirt floor. There was scrap in piles. Bird droppings coming off the rafters. Half of Whitewoman County blowing through the cracks when the wind was up. Cats leaving of themselves. Grease on everything. Sparks flying so fast Clayton didn't even know I was there when I'd stop by to tell him one thing or another. Or the last time I went there. To tell him Casey died.

The Pastor Harrison had tracked me down in Cottonwood because the sheriff had called him. I drove back along the highway to the shed. It was winter, and it was blowing snow off the ground from some weather we'd had the week before. I could see there were no trucks but Clayton's parked out front. Levi was in the cab.

Sometimes when I'd go by in the mornings on my way to Cottonwood I'd see trucks and rigs in front. I'd see Clayton welding on a piece of machinery, the men standing around waiting for him to get done. At least I knew where he was. And he always brought his money home, I'll give him that. The bottle hadn't gotten him either. Thanks be to Jesus.

The time I stopped to tell him about Casey, Clayton didn't know I was in the shed, and I didn't make any noise or come around to where he could see me, or let Levi out of the truck as a sign. I just stood there until he saw me. Maybe ten minutes. He upped his welding helmet and looked at me, and he knew there was trouble. The way we looked at each other.

After I told him about Casey he shut the shed door, snapped the lock, and never went back. It didn't make sense then and it doesn't make sense now. We'd get people coming by the house with welding to do, and he wouldn't do it. Just say no and shake his head. The phone would ring about some job and he wouldn't do it. With spring coming and planters and stock trailers and branding chutes needing work, they'd have to take their jobs to Cottonwood, and the man there cost twice as much and wasn't half as good. The shed sat empty. Still does. I don't wonder what happened to the cats. They didn't come to Bly. I shoot cats to keep them off my birds.

When we got back from Denver, Clayton didn't do anything for work. Not a thing. Only, cut wood the rest of that year to keep us warm. Made me turn off the floor furnace. Cleaned out the flue pipe for the Riverside and got it fired up. I never thought I'd have to use that wood stove again. It seemed like going backward. Here we had a good floor furnace that didn't make a mess, and the co-op delivered the propane. Now I had ashes to clean up and the dirt he'd bring in with the wood. And bugs as well. What a mess. He cut wood all that winter.

Then the next year he cut more wood than we needed. Said he had to lay in two years' supply. Then he went past that. All the time cutting and stacking wood. With him not welding, we lived on what I made cleaning houses in Cottonwood. It's what I've been doing all these years. I'd use the money as savings or for myself and the church. But with Clayton only cutting wood we had to live on it. That's not what I had in mind. I'm getting old. I want a soft life here at the end, with not so many worries as when we started out. I want to be warm in winter, but not with wood.

"What's with Clayton?" says my sister when she sees he isn't going back to the welding shed, and the yard is filling up with stove wood.

"Something to do with Casey," I say.

"How she died?" says my sister. She wants to know, but I haven't told her.

"Just that she's dead," I say.

"I'll pray for her, Only don't tell the Pastor Harrison. He says we're not to pray for the dead. That's what the Catholics do."

"OK," I say.

"Men are strange," she says. "Albert was strange."

"Yes." She was helping me with my bird feeders.

I've decided I'm going to tell about Casey. Why she's buried in Denver. I've decided not to keep that promise. Only I'm going to tell it later. I want to figure out what part comes first. There are two parts. How she lived. How she died. I have to think about it. Maybe telling about Clayton like I promised, it will come to me how to tell about Casey. We'll see.

Clayton wouldn't sell the wood he'd cut. Even after we had more than two years' supply. He'd just cut it and split it and bring it back to Bly. I'd see him head off in the mornings with his truck and his log splitter hitched behind, and his gas cans for his chain saws and the chain saws themselves and Levi all in the back bouncing out of Bly toward the River Road. He'd have packed himself a lunch and a jug of water for himself and one for the dog as well. He'd be gone past sundown. When he'd come home he'd have a pickup full of wood to unload and stack. Which he'd do. Even if he did it in the dark. He worked headlights to headlights. I'll give him that. Do it all, do it now. That was one of his sayings. He was a quiet man. Tall. Grew a beard after Casey died. I came out white.

He'd get just as dirty cutting wood as when he worked in the welding shed. Worse. Only he wouldn't shower in the canning house. Turned his head no when I told him to. Maybe you could talk him out of no when he'd say it, but not when he'd turn his head. He'd strip to his underwear in the backyard and shake out his jeans and work shirts before he'd come into the mudroom where he'd get the rest of the way naked. In winter he'd have on long johns. At least he wasn't so dirty naked. I'd wash his clothes Saturday night, the same as before. Clean for Jesus on Sunday. Not that Casey being dead or cutting wood all week brought him closer to God.

"Good thing Mrs. Harvey moved to Denver," my sister says. She's talking about Clayton getting down to his underwear in the backyard and how Mrs. Harvey was always looking out for something to spread around the church. She's with her daughter now which is one stop before the old folks' home. The Raisin Ranch, Clayton used to call it. Promise me you'll not put me in the Raisin Ranch. Promise now.

"Can you see Clayton from where you are?" I ask.

"If there's enough light."

"Can you tell he's near naked?"

"Not so," says my sister. She's probably telling the truth.

We own most of Bly. When he was in a good mood, Clayton used to say we were Mr. and Mrs. Donald Trump of Bly, Kansas. We own it because everybody's moved out, and before they'd go, Clayton'd buy the house dirt cheap from what he'd saved by himself and whatever lots they wanted to sell. Some people would sell the lots but keep the house in case they lost work wherever they were going. Denver mostly. Kansas City and Wichita as well. The Hustons went to Manhattan. Not New York Manhattan, but Kansas Manhattan. Nobody comes back. By now we own thirty-nine lots and seven houses. Most all the town. I guess I'm the widow Donald Trump of Bly, Kansas. What we don't own my sister does. More or less.

When we'd buy a house, I'd clean it. To keep the mice out, Clayton would find a black snake. They're better than cats. Mostly there wasn't much furniture, only sometimes chairs and broken tables. Televisions. They get left behind when people move. I'd haul the junk to the dump and put the house in some kind of order, only mainly it was just empty space. I like a house when it's empty. There's something about it.

After I was done cleaning, we'd drain the water and lock the door. Always I'd put curtains up so nobody could look in. It just seemed better that way. Maybe word got around about the houses being empty, but nobody wants to live in Bly. We got dirt streets and bad water. Nobody ever wanted to buy one of our houses. No matter how neat they looked. Not that they were for sale.

Clayton stacked his wood on our lots. You could see it on the ten lots we've got to the south of us, and you could see it elsewhere. On the lots where we owned the houses so it looked like someone was living there. On the three lots we own west of my sister's that go right up to the graveyard. On the lots next to the few houses we don't own. The whole of Bly got filled with Clayton's wood.

He'd stack it between trees with lodge pole pine laid down so the wood was kept off the ground. And he always stacked it in a rick so the air would come up and cure it over time. Clayton cut nothing but ash. No cottonwood. Ash. Maybe fifty cords of good split ash before he started trading it. Real neat. The whole of Bly was as neat as my house.

After a while his wood was the main thing about Bly. That and wild turkeys that must be a flock of fifty by now. Also cats people drop off. They'll be in the trees in the mornings after the coyotes come through at night, and I can shoot them better then. I use a .22. It's Clayton's Marlin, but I bought my own shells. Long rifle hollow points. He didn't know about me shooting the cats. Or about me shooting the unworthy birds coming to my feeders. Starlings mainly. For them I use bird shot. Ellen shoots unworthy birds as well. Neither of us shoots the squirrels even though if you don't put out corn cobs they can eat you out of house and home. Once our shooting brought the sheriff to Bly.

"What'd Leo want?" my sister asks. She had gone up to the church to do some typing for the Pastor, and when she came back she saw the Sheriff leaving.

"Told him I was just shooting cats," I say.

"Somebody call in?" she asks.

"Yes, but he won't say who."

"Wendy Thomas," says my sister. She's probably right.

Beyond what we own, the rest of Bly is down to five lived-in houses, unless you count the Stevensons south of town camped out in the old school building. But I don't count them because first of all they're not from around here, and also I don't think they're married. My sister says they do drugs. For sure they raise rabbits because the rabbits are all the time getting out and Levi is all the time killing them so I find a dead rabbit half-chewed in the back yard when I put the clothes on the line. The Stevensons never ask about it though. You'd think they would, but they're trash. He doesn't do any work that I know of.

"They keep a light on all night in that old garage behind the school," says Ellen. "I think he's growing drugs in there. Why else would you not turn off a light?"

"None that I can think of," I say.

"I fed three cardinals this morning," she says. "And my nuthatch came back."

"Did I hear you shoot?"

"Bluejay," my sister says. "Dead."

We buy our birdseed in bulk at the co-op when I go to Cottonwood to clean houses. The same place we get our shells. The rest of us in Bly are related, my sister and her dead husband being the next of relations to me and Clayton. At least to me. The others are shoestring relations to Clayton. That would be Tom Jenkins and his mother-in-law, Wendy Thomas, who lives with him since his wife died. Wendy's always got a gripe about something. She's Episcopalian. They think they've got more manners than other Christians. Then there's Ed Earl Thomas who's not directly related to Wendy Thomas. He's always been a bachelor and is retired from the county roads. Next to him is Mrs. Watkins who claims she lived in three sod houses before she had a frame one. She's a liar. There are days when I think she's dead she sits so still on her porch. I remember when she smoked a pipe. She doesn't have religion and is proud of it. She'll see when she's dead. The devil will smoke her in his pipe. Up near the graveyard there's only my sister, whose Albert is dead five years by now. Some say she shot him, but she didn't. He shot himself and it was an accident. He's buried here in Bly. So is Clayton. In the church graveyard. Not in the county cemetery like he asked for. It's the first promise I didn't keep. You got to start somewhere.

"If he's not in the Great Beyond like he always said he wouldn't be," says Ellen, "then what difference does it make to him where he's planted? Same with Albert. It's us that's living, and us that knows they're buried with the blessing of Jesus."

"It does make me feel better," I say.

"Death is for the living," says my sister. "And besides, "if Clayton is with the Lord, he'll forgive you for what you've done. They teach them that in heaven."

One Sunday afternoon someone from Cottonwood was driving through Bly and came to the door.

"You the man with all this wood?"

"I guess," says Clayton.

"What you want for a pickup load?"

I'm in the kitchen but I can hear.

"I don't sell it," says Clayton.

"It's not cottonwood, is it?" says the man.

How he could say such a thing shows he's from town. You

can tell cottonwood from ash a quarter section away.

"Ash," says Clayton.

"How come you stacked it like you did? Crossways. If I get a pickup worth, I don't want it cross-stacked like that but laid out flat. And piled high. What would you want for such a load?"

"It's not for sale," says Clayton.

"Why not?" says the man. "Looks to me like you got plenty."

When I don't hear Clayton say anything for a long time, I go look. They are on the sidewalk that leads to our front gate. That's when I see the Buick and the wife in it, and I know that they are from down the street of a house I clean in Cottonwood. I know something else about him, but even after they leave I don't tell Clayton. Never did.

"I'll pay your price," says the man.

I see he's backing toward the gate like he thinks Clayton might be a quart low. He probably knows the story about Albert shooting himself, as it made the paper in Cottonwood. Maybe he thinks we're all a quart low here in Bly. Guns going off now and then. People not married to each other living in the old school, a light on all night. Wood all over town. Maybe he knows Tony's our son. Maybe by now he's heard stories of the One-Man Woodcutter working the Whitewoman all by himself, even in summer with only his dog in the truck. I can see Levi's killed another of the Stevensons' rabbits, and he's chewing on it in front of the Buick.

"I'll make a trade," says Clayton just as the man turns through the gate.

"What?"

"I'll make a trade."

"What kind of trade?" says the man from the other side of our fence.

"What you got?" says Clayton.

I'm not happy about what I'm hearing. We don't need anything in trade. That always comes to junk. We need money. More money than I make cleaning houses in Cottonwood, or once a week for that Cody homosexual living by himself in Blaze. We need money, I've said that to Clayton. I let a month go by with him not going back to the welding shed, but when the bank account was getting thin and me taking my cleaning money straight to Food Bonanza for what we need, I told him he ought to get back to welding. But he wouldn't say anything. Just shook his head no.

"Not much that you'd want," says the man. By now he's standing on the sidewalk next to his Buick. He looks at Levi eating the rabbit.

"Think on it," says Clayton.

"Who was that?" my sister says later that afternoon. Clayton is walking the lots checking his stacks. He does that Sundays. The houses, too.

"Somebody from Cottonwood," I say.

"What'd he want?"

"To buy the wood."

"Clayton selling?"

"No," I say. "Says he'll make a trade."

"Just what you need," she says. "Do you know them?"

"I know his car isn't always parked at his house," I say.

"I see."

The part of Clayton's story I'm supposed to tell is how he was on a ship at Pearl Harbor and how he didn't even know what a welding torch was until somebody on December 7th, 1941, handed him one with all the bombs going off and the ship sinking and he was supposed to cut through a metal door so the sailors screaming and banging on the other side could get out. And that's what he did even though he didn't know what he was doing, being even too young to be in the Navy, only he lied about his age. That's the story. But he liked to tell it with the moral of it as well. That you don't know what you can do until you do it.

Clayton never told the story to be a hero. I'll give him that. Only to get to the moral. But he'd put in all kinds of details that I've left out. How everybody was screaming. Blood everywhere. Fire. Water coming in. Men's names, and if they were officers or not. Who died right then and there. All kinds of things I'd see the men around here nod to because they'd been in the war and knew what Clayton was talking about. It was the most he'd talk in one stretch.

He told the story to Tony when Tony came home from Vietnam and lived with us a few weeks before he moved down to Big Oxbow on Cody's ranch. Tony had heard it all before and didn't want to hear it again. He and Clayton had it out about something. I never knew what. Tony came to Clayton's service, though. Not the church service but the burial. I haven't seen him since. He's been by himself to see Casey's grave. That's what I hear. My sister says he was once here in Bly to look at Clayton's grave, but he didn't stop by.

When those sailors got out from behind the door, they remembered Clayton and for years would write him. Not a thank you, but just a note to ask how he was and to say what they were doing. He'd always write back. But whenever they had some kind of reunion, he'd beg off. Clayton made me promise I'd let what was left of them know he was dead. This was one of the promises he got out of me on the Whitewoman after I found him. And a second time in the back of Tony's truck on the way to the hospital in Cottonwood. It wasn't the last promise he got out of me. That was not telling about Casey. But it was the promise next to last. Tell the men I'm dead.

The Sunday after the man with the Buick came to Bly, he

came again, only this time with his truck. Not a truck like we've got in the country, but a sweet new-paint-fever truck, all black with arm rests between the seats and a phone plugged into the cigarette lighter and no dents in it anywhere. He must have kept it in his garage. Not once did I see it in front of his house when I was cleaning for this woman up the street. I was putting out feed for my worthy birds when he drives up. Clayton was walking around Bly looking at his wood and checking our houses. When I see the sweet truck and know who it is, I look to find Clayton. But Clayton sees him as well and comes over and they talk for a moment, but I can't hear so I walk over myself just when Clayton looks into the bed of the truck. I can't see what's there from where I'm standing.

"You can have them all," says the man. "Would that be a fair trade for a load of wood?"

"Where'd you get them?" says Clayton.

"In-laws," says the man. "They went to Mexico a number of years ago and brought them back. I won't say they paid much, but they might be worth something now."

I'm trying to guess what might be in the truck. I know I can't stop what's going on, but I'll have my say later. If you get at them afterward, sometimes it will slow them down next time. That's my sister's idea, too. Not that it ever worked on Albert. Which she says is how he shot himself. Being stubborn about keeping a loaded gun in the house when she'd chew on him not to.

"OK," says Clayton.

The man lowers the tail gate, and I can see there are five round metal light wheels, the kind you hang from ceilings. Like wagon wheels, only not as big. They are mainly black. There are sockets in them for light bulbs, and wires coming out of the hub on top. Around where the light bulbs screw in there are metal leaves. Like off a plant. These are green. There are metal brackets that look like vines. They are green as well, only a darker green. I have come up to the truck. Neither the man nor Clayton says anything to me.

"OK," Clayton says again.

I don't understand what I'm hearing. That was just the beginning.

"What'd you get this time?" my sister says. She always comes over after she sees Clayton's made a trade. By now he's made half a dozen. Two months of Sundays. Various folks. Word was getting around.

"The man said they were Hummels," I say.

"Funny looking little people, aren't they? she says. "And so many all lined up. The case might be worth something."

We are standing outside because it's warm with summer coming in. I am putting out sunflower pods I get from the Pastor's wife. My sister and I feed our birds all the year; that way we get them to nest here in Bly. Just like Clayton's got his wood stacked all over town, we got bird feeders on the lots as well. I tend the ones at my end, my sister tends the ones at her end. You know how some towns got a sign that says they are a tree town or a flower town, well my sister and I want Bly to be a bird town. We talk about making our own sign but can't decide if it should be Bly's for Birds or Bly, Bird Town USA. We agreed on a sign that says Bly Is A Cat-Free Zone, but we could never get either Albert or Clayton to make it for us.

"They take up less space than the lights we got right at the start," I say about the Hummels.

"There's that advantage," she says. "Where's he going to put them?"

"One house or the other," I say. "I never know. Not until I look when he's gone. "

"He still won't sell the trades either?" my sister asks.

"No."

Every Sunday since Clayton died, I've written one of the men on his ship to tell them. At first I'd just write a postcard to save the cost of a first-class stamp, but since Easter I've had more to say about how he died. There are sixteen men on the list that I think are still alive. There were twenty-nine he let out from behind the door. I got four to go. Two have come back with deceased stamped on them. One man's wife, Jane Wiggins Osborne from Wilmer, Minnesota, wrote to say her husband had died in a car wreck because he was half-blind and too stubborn not to drive even though he couldn't get his license re-upped. She went on two pages about all this and what misery it was to live with Mr. Osborne when he got half-blind and stubborn. It was her letter that got me writing more about how Clayton died. Only I haven't answered her back. I'm thinking on it. Maybe she's the one I'll tell about Casey. I think I will.

Just now I'm writing a letter to a Robert W. Boyd of Old Town, Maine. He's the last one on the list. I've made a copy of it in pencil, and when I get it the way I like, I'll have my sister type it out. She used to be a secretary. In it I've told how Clayton didn't come home one Saturday at noon like he said he was because he wanted to be here to make another trade for the wood. Usually Clayton would only make his trades on Sunday, but this was an exception. I didn't know why.

When Clayton didn't show up after an hour, the man left. I didn't like him, and I didn't like what he had to trade. A collection of Coke bottles with the names of the towns where they were made stamped on the bottom. Also, an old Coca-Cola sign. I knew Clayton would have made the swap, so I was glad he wasn't home.

Then I had a vision. I was cleaning my bird feeder and I had a vision that something was wrong. It was a green-black thing in my mind. The color you get at the bottom of clouds that have tornadoes in them. There was a sound as well, a kind of hissing sound. Not like a snake. Not like anything I've heard.

That's when I got in my car.

The River Road goes along the Whitewoman River from Bly to Blaze, and I knew that's where Clayton had been cutting. About ten miles east toward Blaze I saw his truck. Levi wasn't in the back or even in the cab. I could see where Clayton had been working, but I couldn't see him. Then I heard Levi barking. I couldn't see where he was. Just hear him. Then I found them both.

That's as far as I've gotten in my letter to Robert W. Boyd of Old Town, Maine. It's taken a page and a half, front and back, and I want to end it, but I don't know how much I need to tell about going over the fence and then down the river where I find Clayton with Levi barking over him. And the big dead limb I had to pull off him. Or if I ought to say about how Clayton was awake when I found him, but that he'd pass out. And the rest of it. The blood all over his head and down into his eyes. And Tony coming along by chance and how we loaded Clayton into the back of Tony's truck and took him to the hospital with me riding with him in the bed and Levi chasing the truck until we left him behind and that he didn't come home for two days. In the postcards, I'd just write: "Clayton died not long ago cutting wood. A widowmaker got him. He wanted you to know." My sister didn't even have to type them. But telling more about how he died takes more than a postcard.

I don't see why Clayton made me promise about Casey. What people don't know, just means they'll make it up. Most of what you hear isn't true. Clayton was all the time saying that to me when I'd tell him one thing or another about people here in Bly, or the women I clean for in Cottonwood. Nothing much is true, is what he'd say. But others make it up worse than me. And if you don't tell them something, then they make it all up. To this day I don't know what people are saying about how Casey died. They never tell you, just like I never tell Stevenson I think he deals drugs and that he's not married to his wife. But in his case I'm right about what I think, so that's not making it up.

Word got around about the trades Clayton made for wood, and before long we had not only those black wheel lights, but a set of mounted wall maps of the world from years ago to now, that case of Hummels, ten Winchester wooden cartridge boxes, three Negro men statues holding out a ring in their hands as if that's where you're to tie a horse, a barbed wire display with the names and dates of all kinds of barbed wire written below the wire itself, a set of four saddles arranged in a row on saddle stands with the first saddle only being the tree and the rest of saddles getting more to them so you can see how a saddle is made. Everything a set of some kind because Clayton wouldn't trade for anything that was just one of a kind or boxes of junk. I'll give him that.

He'd put what he traded for in our houses or, like the Negro men, into the yards. On Sundays he'd walk around Bly looking at his wood and going into the houses to check on his collections. It wouldn't be until later that I'd learn what he got. And then only because after he'd leave Monday mornings, I'd go over to the house where he'd put it and see what it was.

The Sunday before he died, he'd traded for three big photographs of old cowboy bands, all blowed up and mounted. Framed real neat. But who wants to look at a picture of the Dodge City Cowboy Band from God knows when? Clayton and me, we never talked about these trades. Just like we never talked about him not going back to work, or how he'd just cut more and more wood all by himself, so that it wasn't long before my sister said he's called the One-Man Woodcutter of the Whitewoman. We never talked about any of it.

"There's something you're not telling me about Casey," says my sister the Sunday after Pastor Wilbur preached a sermon on Casey being such a special girl and how we'll miss her, but that she was with her eternal Father now and that should give us satisfaction. Clayton wouldn't go, even though he knew what the sermon would be because the Pastor had stopped by to grieve with us.

"I can't," I say.

"Can't what?" my sister says.

"Can't tell you."

"Clayton make you promise?"

"He did."

"OK." she says. But she asks me about it anyway every time we visit. Sometimes hinting. Sometimes straight out.

"Clayton let you off that promise yet?"

"No."

"Can you say why she's buried in Denver and not here?"

"No."

Once, Clayton went to Denver by himself. He never told me. Only since he wasn't dirty, I asked him what he did that day. Then he told me. Took Levi with him. Denver and back. Five hundred miles round trip. We didn't talk about it. The next day he went back to cutting wood. The Sunday after that is when he traded for the Negro men.

I'm going to Denver myself. Later this summer. When I get all Clayton's men written. But I need to take my sister so we can share the driving. I'm getting old. I'll grieve one more time at Casey's grave, and that will be the end. Once for both me and Clayton when we buried her. Once for Clayton by himself, and once for me. Then there's Clayton's grave here in Bly. All this death and my own coming along. Everything dying out with nobody left in the country, not even so many in Blaze anymore, and the butane stars we used to see on the farms at night now gone. More people in the graveyards than in church these days. And maybe them buried with something they didn't tell. What secrets should you go to your grave with? That's what I want to know.

Even though Clayton's dead, I still got people from Cottonwood coming out on Sundays to make trades for the wood. I say no to trades. I sell it. He didn't make me promise not to sell it, so I do. I get a hundred dollars a full pickup load, stack it yourself the way you want it and as high as you want. The stacks are going down. We still got turkeys and birds and dirt streets and bad water and sometimes cats in the trees, but we've got less wood. Times are changing.

I'm also selling what Clayton traded it for. I get a few buyers. Antique dealers off the highway come down because they've gotten wind of what's here. I show them around. The Hummels went first. Then one of the Negro men. The wagon-wheel lights are still here. The cartridge boxes got me a good price.

"I want one of those Negroes holding a horse ring," says my sister. "For my front yard." I have been shooting unworthy birds, and she's heard me so she's come up.

"Sure," I say.

"Are they too heavy for the two of us to carry?"

"I think we can manage," I say.

"You want to go to Clayton's grave?" she says.

"Today?"

"I was thinking of visiting Albert," she says.

"Let's move the Negro first."

And we do. I take the ring in his hand and my sister takes his feet. We walk down Middle Dirt to her house and put him at the end of her driveway, next to the cattle skull that's there.

"He looks good," my sister says, backing up to take him along.

"He does," I say. Then we walk over to the graveyard.

I've had another vision. All my life I've had visions. Not many. But some. Right after I got married there was a blue ball at my feet in bed just before dawn, and I guessed it was God, but He didn't say anything, and as the morning came it started to turn pale so I could see the wall behind it, and when Clayton turned on the light in the bedroom to get dressed it was gone. I never told Clayton about it. Or Ellen either. I told Casey, though.

I don't always see things in my visions. Sometimes I just feel them. Even if I don't see anything, I still call it a vision. I think maybe if I stay with it long enough and peer into what I'm feeling, something will show up. This new one is following me.

When I'm walking through town checking on my bird feeders and the houses and what's left of Clayton's wood, it's been at my back. It doesn't scare me. Not like the black-green cloud that told me Clayton was hurt. This is something soft following me. I turn around and try to look into it. But I don't see anything. It's been with me most of the week. I haven't told Ellen. But I told Clayton. At his grave. Not the other day when I went with my sister after we moved the Negro, but yesterday.

"Is that you, Clayton?" I say. I am standing at his feet.

It has been warm in recent days. Not yet hot, but getting there. The wheat harvest is on. That makes the sunsets red. I go to the edge of Bly to watch them. The vision is with me then. When night comes, it leaves. Then it comes back in the morning and follows me, but only when I go outside. It's not with me in the house.

"Is that you, Clayton?" I say again. Levi has found me. He's wet from having been in the creek or somebody's stock tank.

When he shakes, it goes over Clayton's stone.

"I'm sorry I put the cross on your stone," I say to Clayton.

"I just didn't feel right not doing it. If that's you following me, give me a sign."

Then I think it's not Clayton, it's Casey. Or maybe it's one of the men from Clayton's ship. Or maybe it's all of them from the ship that he saved but now are dead, and what they're trying to tell me is that he's with them. And Casey is, too. I peer around me to see what I can see.

"Give me a sign," I say.

Levi thinks I'm talking to him and sits down. I can feel the vision is all over me. Front and back and it's rising out of the ground. It feels good. It's like harvest sunsets or a hunter's moon. Maybe it's my own time come to get me. But I haven't been sick. And I've chores to do. Clayton left me his social security, but I still clean a few houses in Cottonwood. There's the wood and the trades to sell off. The floor furnace to get the Co-Op man to clean before fall comes. Maybe Tony and I will have time together now that everybody's gone but the two of us. Maybe he'll tell me what happened between him and Clayton. Sometimes I'm tired. But I've got my birds to feed. It can't be my time has come.

"Who's there?" I say.

My sister comes out of her house and calls to me something I can't understand. The vision goes away. Not that I think it's angry, just that it wants to be with me and nobody else.

It's about Casey. I've thought on it. I'm not going to tell. I want Clayton to have that. I don't want him to be the One-Man Woodcutter who died for nothing. Not that I ever understood him. I never knew what any of it was about. Not the promises. Cutting the wood. The trades. How the shed on the highway is still locked, and by now I've lost the key. That he wouldn't shower in the canning house after Casey died. Or why he wouldn't go meet those men whose lives he saved. Why he grew his beard. It's what I just finished writing to Mrs. Jane Wiggins Osborne of Wilmer, Minnesota. That I never understood what Clayton did, but now that he's been dead long enough for me to think on it, I'm not going to tell her about Casey. Not to anybody. Not to Ellen. Only to Jesus when my time comes. But that will be to give me peace even though Jesus knows how Casey died. I'll be with her then. And maybe with Clayton, too. I hope so. Now that he's dead, I hope so. The letter, it took me a page front and back. I wrote by hand and didn't have my sister type it.

It's in the mail.

Pan-Kansas Swimming Champion

Swim Date, Ten Laps

I am sitting in the locker room remembering that the television doctor told me to stop thinking about my body as a bag into which my organs and bones have been stuffed. Nor should I imagine it as the biology book overlays of my fifties high school general science class: the static electricity slapping the thin plastic pages of Veins and Arteries onto Bones and Cartilage in such a way that a fatal crease runs from the superior mesenteric to the subclavian. Such transparent geography is wrong these days. Old maps. Old bags of bones. Wrong mind set.

I was assured by my morning colleague in the glass that we should now see our body as a plethora of waters: creeks and streams and oxbows. Lakes and ponds and marshes. With banks and beds, and now and then small dams—wanted or unwanted. "We are," he said, leaning toward me as if in a consultation, "an ecosystem of fluids through which run ridges of minerals and rills of electricity. Drink water, be water: how we conceive ourselves matters."

To reconceive myself, I have started a lunchtime swim as a way to skip the country club's diabetic buffet. No doubt my television doctor would approve, just as I would approve such a regime for my own patients. However, I want more than health for my laps. I want to swim myself backward through time.

I want to see myself slimmer, younger, stronger as the water washes past. In a previous age, I was Bobby Brown playing third base for the New York Yankees. I was as well the Pan-Kansas swimming champion. Wouldn't it be pretty to think so.

In a moment of exertion after the exhaustion of my first swim, I am trying for a watery conception. The best I can do is to conjure the thunderhead of my heart beating over the newly washed prairie of my smokeless lungs. The panorama of my mind fills with base paths and line drives; instead of the plethora of waters there is a field of 1950s New York Yankees: Mantle, Maris, Berra. Some part of my body that I do not recognize becomes an eternal Italian centerfield. The thunder of my heart turns to applause. It is early October and a towering drive to left becomes larger the farther it sails. From an unlocatable bleacher I watch my game being played out: The baseball—now as bright as a summer midnight moon—clears the fence, and I vanish, only to find myself looking with the redness of my eyes at the puddle below my bench. I try to recover a vision of myself—my body, my ball field—by going back to it through my ears. Instead of applause, I hear the faint ring of a tiny mechanical insect: Tinnitus. It is the sound of ear nerves dying. A part of hearing lost in its own death cry: the essence of irony.

There are more kinds of irony than there are names for it. Or nerves dying so, while the dream of my new self has been hit over the fence, and yet another insect is cranking up to die in my other ear; I feel pretty good. Not like clear bays or brisk running creeks. Not like a crisp double play. But not bad. I drain my newly bought "water caddy." Life is good.

Swim Date, Twelve Laps

That's a third of a mile in the pool where I swim. A college pool. Up to the College, we say in town. The man with the locker next to mine, a Mr. Taylor (it is he who uses the Mister for himself) explains the nomenclature of our swimming.

"A length is up," he says. "A lap is up and back. It takes thirty-six laps to make a mile. Mr. Taylor is up to a mile. Even though we are newly retired. And we know what that means. Agewise."

We wonder what business Mr. Taylor practiced that robbed him of his first person. Or if he shed it like some skin along the way only to grow another against new visions of mortality. We have seen him now and then around town and at large parties, but we do not circle in the same smaller circles.

Mr. Taylor tells me that I need a pair of goggles. In my youth I swam the municipal pools of Kansas with my eyes awash and open. The world then wasn't red and blurry when I got done. Nor was my skin dry. It was probably all that iodine and baby oil. Either that, or—as we learned in medical school—I am drying from the inside out. ("The skin is an organ," the professor of dermatology made us repeat out loud three times the day he visited one of our classes.) A body that was once a vibrant sea has given way to a swamp that is turning into a marsh that will turn into an alluvial plain with tiny flowers going to seed. (I must remember not to talk to my patients in extended metaphors.) But Mr. Taylor is right: I need goggles. I need skin balm (some sample sizes of an ammonium lactate I have at the office). I need earplugs.

"And time on your side," Mr. Taylor says. You need time on your side as well. Something we don't have. "How did we do today?" he inquires.

Like a truculent patient who won't confess to the number of cigarettes he smokes a day, I won't tell him exactly how we did: "Not bad," I say.

In truth there *was* some flaccidity in the legs, as if our kick *were* not connected to our stroke. At eight laps we wanted to quit, but we threatened ourselves with the horror of a long-gliding airplane crash if we didn't swim on. It is an old device of ours. We dream up a superstition to suit the moment: Don't make the morning rounds and get lymphoma. Don't see the hypochondriac wife of the mayor, and the television hurricane will bend up the bay and sink the sailboat. Such mental violence is what is left of our Puritan Ethic. Tomorrow we fly to Kansas City. Medical School Reunion. As we turned into lap nine, we saw our plane climb back to altitude.

"We tried jogging and this is better," says Mr. Taylor. "Too much jarring of the bones in jogging," he says, as he goes through the door to the pool so that his voice echoes. Jarring bones. Bones. Bones. It is as if he takes up our laps where we have left off.

We all agree, even though we are beginning to feel uncomfortable in Mr. Taylor's persona and that of our morning medical man. Tense and person. Bays and bones. Water, water everywhere. Balls and strikes. Mainly strikes today: fastballs belt high that reduce our reflexes to a flinch. We pack our cell phone and drive to the clinic.

Swim Date, Eight Laps

Yogi Berra's number.

Kansas City was cold. But bright and windless. I took an afternoon off and went down to McGee where the old ballpark had been. I once saw Berra play third base there. The Kansas City Blues were a farm team for the Yankees, and every summer they would come to town and play out of their positions: Rizzuto at first base. Jerry Coleman in right field. Ralph Houk in left. Micky Mantle at shortstop.

As I did lap seven, I thought about some X rays of Mantle's badly torn anterior cruciate ligament I'd once seen in a journal and how now it could be repaired, but then it could not so the "fastest man to first" played for years in bandaged pain.

I thought about how he played shortstop in Joplin where I first set up practice. I thought about his father teaching him to hit left-handed, and about how I kept a Louisville Slugger 32/34 in my office in those days so I could practice my swing between patients, standing in front of a mirror I had on the back of my door and hitting mostly from the left side.

As I came into the turn halfway through lap seven, I watched Mantle make his drag bunt to the right side of the diamond and race toward first. I picked up my pace; I hustled the ninety feet. My hand touched the side of the pool. Safe. Mantle turns toward the stands, his number rippling on his back, his effort to stop etched in his face. The crowd is ablaze with applause in the late July sun. We are all applause.

Coming back down seven, I laid my body out in the water in front of me and notice someone coming up beside me. A girl. A young woman. Black tank suit. The flutter of her kick drives her past me.

I swim up Berra's number toward Maris and Rizzuto—and an obscure infielder named Jerry Lumpe—none of whom I reach. I finish awash in bad ball hitting and only modest satisfaction. The girl has passed me coming and going.

Mr. Taylor is heading for two miles. "We are pleased with our one-mile accomplishment, so we are going to make our advance toward two miles beginning tomorrow. We are going to add a lap a day for a week, then level off for a week. A plateau at forty-two. Then forward again."

Inside Mr. Taylor's locker, there is a strip of white adhesive tape running lengthwise, on which he has some kind of marking system. He peels off an old tape full of cross-hatched lines and lays in a new one. There is a small wrinkle in it, which he notices and fixes by popping the tape off and laying it back on again, smoothly.

"Mrs. Taylor is no longer with us," he says. She has gone to Florida. He closes the locker and leaves.

Swim Date, Twelve Laps

The goggles make it all clear. I especially like the patch of sunshine in the deep end that comes through the window of the pool to the west and lays itself down along the bottom like a slab of white chocolate. Then there are the bubbles from the turns: how buoyant they are. A trail of my previous self through which for a moment I swim. The bubbles thin out by the time I've coasted to the end of my push-off, and then I am into the clear water of the new me. "All of three," I say to myself in order to keep track of what lap I am on. All of three. Even as I am thinking all of four. "All of three."

When I was younger, I did the tumble turn at the end of the lengths, where you duck your head just before you touch the edge of the pool and then twist so your feet wind up flat against the side. The trick is to turn and push all in the same motion. It isn't difficult to do, but to do it now would mean I'd lose a breath—and the sense of rhythm I need to get to all of twelve. Everything in its time. The tumble turn of yesteryear. Clichés are thrilling when you feel good.

Just as I am about halfway through five, I sense a swimmer in the next lane. The girl. She passes me and I follow her in and out of the turn midway through five—but she is fast. And steady. And she comes off the wall before I do. I watch the beat of her feet as they plunge air into the water ahead of me. Then her lane grows calm, her trace engulfed. I thrash on in some kind of silence I hadn't before known, and watch for her to come back up the pool. Which she does.

I see her face as it turns toward me, mouth agape, eyes strangely hollow in their goggles. In my mind's eye I mark the spot where we have crossed to see at what rate she is gaining on me. The next lap we meet nearer the middle, and the lap after that I see her coming into turn seven just as I am going out. It is taking something out of me, but I push myself to stay ahead of her into lap eight.

Going into nine I hear a thud at the surface that tells me she has flipped the turn; I am lapped. I feel taken, and I am surprised at the sensation: lightness and calm, and something blue in my mind for a moment. I watch the trail of bubbles she lays down in front of me. They are becoming smaller, then a froth.

When the water clears, I no longer think of keeping any kind of pace with her. I swim along toward ten through twelve, not marking where we pass but knowing she is lapping me at some rate immeasurable, each lap bringing with it a swell of anxiety and then something like a small nap. All of twelve. All of King Kong Keller and Gil McDougald. All of black tank suit.

"We are going to use the training crawl to get to two miles," says Mr. Taylor. "Do we know the training crawl?"

I say we do, although I have not been using it.

"For the long run you need it," he says. We wish we'd used it from the beginning. There is a pause while we both putter with the gear in our lockers.

"We were watching you just now," Mr. Taylor continues, "and you need to bring your kick up higher." He makes his hands my feet, and beats them in the air above his forehead.

Mr. Taylor is right about my kick, just as I will be right this afternoon when I tell my first patient that he must bring down his weight and cut out salt or he'll explode from the blood-pressure numbers I have threatened to write backward across his forehead so he can see who he is when he looks in the morning mirror: We are how we see ourselves, I will tell him. Drink water. Take no salt before its time.

"You'll do better," Mr. Taylor says, "with your feet up. Up." His hands rise on the beat of them as my feet. Lest he swim backward out the door I assure him we'll do better tomorrow.

My patients are never so quick to assess or value my opinion. They take their advice, I suspect, from someone else—perhaps from the same television doctor I watch in the mornings; or if not from him, then from the business correspondent on the evening news. It amounts to the same thing: Advice is news, and it too shall pass.

Maybe my patients are right in resisting cures that are not pills or shots or surgery. Who am I to tell them about their lives? Some days (today, for one) I think I should keep to my place: Name their malady. Note its history. Describe the length and number of its lap. Tell them it is either self-limiting or fatal.

Then say: "There, there."

Maybe I should try it this afternoon when I read again the chart of my second patient: "There, there." Diabetes: Glucose 200 up from 150. Then all of 250 by this time next year if he doesn't stop drinking his "Industrial Strength Martinis." Think smoke stack, Doc, think "Industrial Strength." ISM for short. Blood pressure all of 170. All of PSA, all of Prostate: all zip. He lost it four years ago to my right index finger and to one of my partner's scalpels. Think moderation, I'll say to ISM.

As for myself, tomorrow I'm going to raise my kick and move my laps to fifteen. When I get to half a mile, I'll make the tumble turn of my youth and sprint for home, Zeus's sperm flying.

I leave the locker room and go into the lobby and look through the glass doors at the pool. The girl in the black tank suit is still swimming, lapping Mr. Taylor at some fantastic rate. Her head is high as she bites the air for breath. Her feet boil the water with the precision of even heat. She seems younger at her age than I was at her age. Beautiful and carnivorous, she swims as if she's after something.

I do not wait to see Mr. Taylor lapped again but walk outside and across the campus. It is early October. Warm as World Series weather.

Swim Date, Zero Laps

To put myself to sleep at night I think of swimming: The placement of my head. The angle of my hands as they break the surface. The trail of bubbles my hand makes before my eyes as I pull it through. The boil of my feet. The glide of the final stroke before the wall. The integrity of laps. Laps. All of dreams. When I was a boy, I'd put myself to sleep by playing third base for the Yankees: Furillo is at bat. I have crept up along the line for the bunt. I nod to Rizzuto at short and to Joe Collins at first. We understand. Reese takes a lead at second. Lopat is on the mound. McDougald is hedging his bets toward Collins. Should the bunt go toward first, I'll break back to cover third. We have done this before; it only takes the slightest gestures among us to make the play.

When Furillo hits the ball down the line, I switch my dream to the radio announcer's play-by-play: Like the drive itself, my dive to catch it is an instantaneous tight rope to the ground. Furillo takes a step toward first then stops dead, head down, in his tracks.

Some nights I am suspended above the third-base line, the white ball smack in my glove. Other nights—after I have hit the dust with the catch—I bolt off the ground and hold the ball up for all to see. Sometimes, it is the end of the inning and my body thumps into the dirt for a moment while the crowd gasps that I might be hurt; then I spring to my feet and walk to the dugout where Casey Stengel ignores me. On nights when there is only one out, I pop to my knees and fire the ball to McDougald, who has come over to second, and we double up Reese in a play that has him stopped in the same state of amazement as is Furillo. The crowd roars. The radio announcer describes it over and over again until the stadium glows with the words.

However, these nights in bed my goggles are fogged and the slab of light at the deep end has a melted quality. My shoulders ache, but my feet have come up (Mr. Taylor approves), and I can see they are driving me. Turning my head, I study the way my arms rise out of the water. I watch the spray of my stroke and imagine I am a camera in charge of perfection. Doc Councilman is reviewing the films and waiting for my body-density charts. I am doing the training crawl: two strokes on one side, one stroke to change over, and two strokes on the other side. Breath, breath, stroke, death, breath. All of looking to sleep on, some second self.

To keep track of my laps I roll over my IRAs one lap at a time. I give the IRA a name: Apollo, Bacchus, and I fill the lap's length by trying to compound the interest until my retirement. It is all further away than my college classics class or my weak math skills can take me. Still (I can hear Mr. Taylor whispering), we must begin somewhere. Besides, there is something gaining on me as I name and number my yields: something slimmer, stronger, younger. It laps me, and I struggle for a moment to the surface of my dreams but do not come awake.
My night's swimming has left me exhausted. I lay off a day. None of today. All of none today.

Swim Date, Fifteen Laps

The other evening I met Edward Albee at a party. The College had invited him to campus. I have not read Albee's famous play, but I've seen the movie. I've see Martha make fun of George

Segal. I heard her call him "Pan-Kansas Swimming Champion."

George Segal and I look alike. I know when he has been on television because the next day my patients will comment on our similarity. It also happens that one of my favorite actresses is Sandy Dennis, Sandy Dennis of *Sweet November.* Mine is bad taste, I know. But there it is.

"Were you satisfied with Taylor and Burton?" asks a professor standing in our small circle by a sideboard of drinks.

"They promised me Brando and Bette Davis," Albee says. He tilts his head and runs his hand along his ear. There is some chatter about this response, but Albee seems distracted. He notices me watching him. He runs his finger around his ear's helix and down into the concha where he makes a small drilling motion.

"A tiny ringing inside the ear," he says. The sign that one of the nerves that collects sounds is dying. He looks at me.

"How did you happen to create George and Martha?" asks the professor. Albee still has my eye; it is as if he has seen me somewhere before. Behind our group, Mr. Taylor, in an Orvis tweed sports coat, is talking to the college president, who is talking to Mr. ISM, who is drinking one.

"Were you satisfied with George Segal and Sandy Dennis?" Albee says to me.

I say very much so. Albee nods. We don't continue because he is swept along in some conversation about theatre of the absurd and talk of Shakespeare and George and Martha.

They promised me DiMaggio and Monroe, I say to myself on lap five—or is it six? Outside an early winter storm has made a mess of the bar of deep-end light. The slate-gray color of the sky is the color of the water. I have lost track of my lengths, and my way of keeping myself honest is to swim another lap for each lap I've forgotten. If I'm on five, but I'm not sure of that, I assume I'm on four—and I'll do five again. In this way I stretch myself.

Into lap six I begin to make divisions. I am halfway to the one-third mark. I swim up seven as a lucky number, and turn all of eight as some numerical cousin to thirty-six. Nine is Maris. Poor dead Roger Maris. Ten will be even. The decimal system. The Bill of Rights. Kilometers. Five-eighths of a mile. The Ten Commandments. I lose track again and go back down the line-up. Poor dead Roger Maris. All of Roger Maris Berra. I punch a low-and-away fast ball down the left field line for a double. All of "Industrial Martinis." Cholesterol at 200, all bad. All of fifteen. And then some.

"We were in kitchens," says Mr. Taylor, as I sit on the bench. We built kitchens from New York to Newport. Our Silver Line Division put kitchens in tract houses, but our Sterling Division did theme kitchens: Italian modern kitchens in black and white with built-in pasta cupboards. French provincial kitchens. Early American kitchens with Flemish Bond brick fireplaces. Oriental kitchens. One guy wanted a Wizard of Oz kitchen. Judy Garland wallpaper. Yellow brick floor. We did it.

Against his locker I see the strip of white tape and a number of black marks. He adds another one and then lays the marking pen on the top shelf from which he fetches something else.

"Lisbon," he says, holding a small plastic bottle for me to see. When I shower today I'll use shampoo we got at the Ritz in Lisbon. My wife in Florida, she packs her bags with all the free soap you can get in hotels. Madrid. Paris. Rome. London. I got it all here." He points to the top shelf of his locker as he puts back Lisbon, then walks into the shower.

As if he is somehow aware of me, my television doctor has recently recommended our swimming. It uses all our muscles. It returns us to the water. It suspends us. It does not pound us.

It helps our fluids circulate. Our blood must run to our capillaries—a corner of the universe where it seldom goes. We must open up small creeks and wash out the litter of the dry beds. The secret to health and long life, he tells the camera that I am beginning to think is located just behind my head, is in both our waters and in the channels in which those waters flow. No wonder I feel better.

Swim Date, One Lap

Water streams into my goggles going up; coming back, I tell myself unless I finish the first lap the price of IBM will drop twenty points by the closing bell. I thrash on to the end and stop. I empty my goggles and press them onto my head with the palm of my hands. I push off for the second lap; the goggles fill again. I stop. Standing in the shallow water about five yards from the pool's edge I tighten the straps. I can't decide if I should go back and push off again or go ahead from where I am. There is no one else in the pool. Only the lifeguard who has run the wires of his iPod up inside of his sweatshirt and who is listening to a different drummer than I am.

I lose track of everything; I can't seem to count backward far enough to make up for the laps I've lost. I wade to the pool's edge, pull myself out and go inside to take a shower. As I leave, I notice the girl in the black tank suit has begun her laps. Alone, she seems bent on besting herself.

Swim Date, All of Twenty

A quantum leap. A point in time. The whole nine yards. Beyond Whitey Ford and Vic Raschi. Out into deep water. The modest achievement of my precious bodily fluids. All done in her presence, all done with her by my side. Many times by my side.

"How did we do today?" asks Mr. Taylor. I notice the tone of his body: papier-mâché white, an old fork break in the left forearm—and that I also have become we. We did all right, we say; we have learned the value of understatement.

At all of eleven, she goes by me going into the far turn. I follow her bubbles out and catch sight of her arches. Her legs and thighs disappear into the agitation of blue-and-white water. I lay back, looking for what kind of pace she has in for me. I am heading for half a mile, while playing a night game in Flatbush.

In Kansas City we do not know what Flatbush means, any more than in our Methodist Youth Fellowship we know the location of the Holy Land that we imagine is east of Florida. Nor do we know why the New York Yankees are called the Bronx Bombers. We tend to believe that "the Bronx" is some kind of secret plane that our *Life Magazine* of World War II book does not show us. With the handles of our bats, we draw the Bronx in the dust of our infield: It has fat wings, a tall tail, four motors, and streams of bombs that drop all around home plate.

Later that night the Yankees play a game in Flatbush. I am Bobby Brown at third base. I go two for four against Chicago: a pair of sharp singles, both up the middle. Not screamers like Bill Skowron will hit, but hard liners hit off good pitches that other batters might curse themselves for watching into strikes.

I have developed this theory that Bobby Brown never hits a bad ball. That he's the hitter who watches for a good pitch and slaps it—that's the word I want—slaps it into right center. Berra can hit all the bad balls he wants; I wait for the waist-high fastball over the fat of the plate in Flatbush, Kansas, as I swim myself down the pool's lane in pursuit of the black tank suit. All of four for four.

I have our pace. She crosses my path three strokes closer to me each time we meet. At fourteen we go into the turn together and I follow her heels halfway until I lose sight of them. The slab of sunlight is set rippling, and I know where she is ahead of me. We cross at two strokes before I come into the turn. Out of the turn I slip back into Flatbush, where I am stationed at my sack, steady and methodical.

I am watching my hand come into the water. Bubbles trail from it; it wavers through its pull. I watch it, my hand, come out, full of spray and droplets as if in a photograph. Beside me, she goes by in the arch of my arm. I feel on cruise control. I turn and head into water I had not intended entering. All of sixteen. The rivers and lakes and bayous of my body hustle to catch up. All of Whitey Ford. All of Bob Cerv. All of Don Larson.

At nineteen, I lose track of what I am doing. I put myself in the on-deck circle, my number six flapping on my back in the desert wind. Studying the pitches, I collect myself. Coming into the far turn at twenty, I remember that I wanted to do my tumble turn; I tuck my head for a moment but think better of it. Something to save for a mile.

When I am playing at Yankee Stadium I am flamboyant. A crowd pleaser. A diver to the left. A diver to the right. But when I am Bobby Brown in Flatbush, I am methodical. I check my spikes for dirt, and I check my leggings to see that the arch of white along the side is what it should be. I touch the bill of my cap. Robinson is up. I see that Berra has called for a curve from Lopat. Of course. This one is down and away, but still Robinson pulls it toward me. A chop that has hit the ground before the pitcher's mound and which is destined to clatter on into left over Rizzuto's outstretched glove until I cut it off and—fielding the half-hop so it doesn't have the chance of a bad bounce—fire it over to Mize at first. All of which I do while keeping myself inside myself. No flip turn. End of the inning. Start of the final lap.

I push off hard. I feel my kick rise in the water. I see it driving me. I stretch my arms. I raise my brow so that the water breaks across my forehead. Doc Councilman, here I come. I am swimming down the lens of the underwater camera. My body-density chart shows that I am lithe in the pools of my dreams. I touch myself out. I am the Pan-Kansas Champion. I take off my goggles and look around. She is all of gone.

Swim Date, The Pool at Night

After the Edward Albee party I walked through the campus to my condo. A fog hung over the lawns; the sidewalk lamplights were confined to lighting themselves. Ahead, I could make out the figures of a faculty couple as they turned down the lane to their campus house. By the intermittent growl of their talking, I concluded they were in a post-party row.

I stopped by the pool. It has large glass sliding doors along two sides, and the front and back doors are glass as well. You can see clear through.

The building was lit in that obligatory nocturnal way: a few lights in various corners and one coming from someplace you could not see. It looked like an Equity lit stage, something an actor might come back to at night just to see one more time before he left the show for good. I went up to the side door and looked in. The water was level, but there were tiny swirls and miniature eddies coming from its circulation. There was nothing to be seen beneath the surface.

Swim Date, 12-32-10

I can't get into my locker. Some set of numbers out of my past has come forward into my head, and I can't unlock my brain to get my present combination. Where must I go in my youth to unlock the lock with the combination I keep dialing? I sit on the bench and probe.

I think of brain scans I saw the other day in a journal. It showed that very smart people solve problems only with the part of the brain that is designed for such functions, but that those less gifted must have their brains search everywhere among the lobes and hemispheres for the solution. I see lights on deep in my fronix. I see that I am aglow along all twelve of my cranial nerves. All of brain. All of memory. A television on from top to bottom and side to side. All of twenty-four inches on the diagonal. We are how we conceive ourselves.

"We're closing in on two miles today," says Mr. Taylor, as he comes into the locker room and notices I am still dressed. We have our rhythm. He pauses. "What's the matter? Forget the combination?" Yes, we say.

"It happens to me," he says. He goes over to a fire extinguisher housed in a crèche in the tile wall and opens the glass door. He tilts the extinguisher away; under it is a small piece of yellow notepaper:

"Twenty-four, eleven, twenty-two. Most of the time I've got the combination right up front" (and here he taps his forehead) "but sometimes not. Today not. When I was younger I could use the twitch system. Do you know the twitch system?"

"No," we say. Mr. Taylor seems to have forgotten it himself as he opens his locker. Oddly, I wonder who his doctor is.

"You can get your combination from the pool staff," he says as he pulls off his clothes. "You don't want to miss your exercise. A day off is a day backward."

Something in me wants to go backward today, so I spin the dial on my lock in the knowledge that the combination is in my desk at the office but that in between patients instead of hitting left-handed into a mirror (something I've taken up again of late), I'll devise a way to remember my numbers. Maybe I'm young enough to use the twitch system, whatever that is. In the end, I'll probably have to open the desk drawer.

Leaving, I notice someone young and lithe and lovely and not yet a black tank suit go into the women's locker room. The sky is gray. Winter is north and west of us.

Swim Date, A Mile

I guess I've done a mile. Early on I lost count, thinking about something I don't recall now and so went back to the last number I remembered. I got through five laps just keeping track of the numbers, and then she slid in beside me and I followed her for a few laps before I had to go back to a number I remembered. From eleven through twenty, I had my rhythm. I counted my strokes and calculated the interest on my IRAs and played baseball and swam up and down the long flat roads of Kansas.

Beyond twenty, I swam Yankee numbers when I knew them; and when I didn't, I put the number on myself and played third base the whole lap, the announcer saying that... "old what's-his-number has done it again, diving to the right to rob Reese of a sure double." It wasn't the same.

Around lap twenty, I began to wonder if I would remember to do my tumble turn on thirty-six. Then I drifted off somewhere and began thinking of the waters inside me and about the ironies involved. I lost track of losing track. I was treading water while keeping pace and heading for all-of-some-number I could not figure. I found myself thinking of a patient who this afternoon will learn from me the nature of his death. Not ISM, as it has turned out.

A splash of feet in front of me going into a far turn snaps me out of it. I remember lap twenty-seven, but I think I'll add a number because surely I must have gone on past my memory. All of twenty-seven, I say to myself as I make the turn. It feels like twenty-seven, gritty and sure of itself. Twenty-seven. I watch my hands hit the water and watch them pause for just a moment, floating almost, before I pull them through again. "How many laps to go?" my patient asks me. "Less than all of nine," I say. Poor Roger Maris.

I start counting down the lineup, while the girl is no doubt counting up; the snap and spray of her youth seems vicious in its vigor. I am diminishing, like some old center fielder trying to catch one last fly ball before he mysteriously pops into the outfield bullpen of middle age. With nothing else to do, I go back down the roster toward the wall: All of Berra. All of Mantle. All of me. All of DiMaggio.

She laps me at Gehrig. I lose track. I do the Iron Man twice. All of ALS. I swim through Ruth, wondering where at my back she is hurrying near. All of Frank Crosetti in the coaches' box. I tumble the turn at the far end of the final lap, and my nose fills and my ears pop. For a moment I am lost. Tiny insects fly out of my head. I see the bubbles of my previous self gathering in front of me and push off through them into the bright fresh water of Billy Martin. All of Billy Martin.

I see myself watching a World Series pop-up. I remember to raise my kick so that it propels me forward. I stretch myself for the length that remains. Blood goes up dry creeks. Oxbows swell with new pride. The infield is clear. No one but me to make the catch. She is closing with precision. Racing forward, my hat flying, my glove at arm's length, I touch her out at the wall to win at home. The radio announcer describes my feat to my teammates in Kansas City. She flips her turn beside me and prowls back up the lane.

"Did we do well today?" asks Mr. Taylor. "We look like we did well. As for ourselves, we are closing in on two miles today and washing with a small hotel soap my wife found for us in

Venice. Well, not Venice exactly, but some island off Venice."

We did well, we say.

"Good," says Mr. Taylor. "We talked to Mrs. Taylor last night and told her we were close to two miles. We are not divorced. We are not even separated. She just lives at our place in Florida during the winter. Never go to Florida in the winter," says Mr. Taylor. He has that look on his face as if an aphorism is...is...somewhere, somehow connected to his advice—but in the end he cannot think of it. We ask if he notices the girl in the black tank suit.

"We do not," he says, and makes another mark on his adhesive tape.

Swim Date, Third Person

It was Mr. Taylor at the end of the rescue squad siren this morning during the television doctor's segment. It was not my call. Nor his.

Ours is a small town, so we share duty at the emergency room. Some nights I sleep over in the Spartan cubicle on the second floor. I rather like it—at least for the few days once or twice a month, the obligation is mine. The room reminds me of my university days, institutional: yellow cinder block, a brown plastic sitting chair, a black-and-white television mounted on the wall (on which I never tune in my colleague.) I can't fully say—beyond my association with my previous undergraduate living—why I find such a meager place pleasing. What I do not like is the medical duty it predicts: farm boy and college fraternity men, drunks with beer-bottle gnashes, indigestion mistaken for a coronary infarction, poison ivy. Nothing my There, there is good at curing.

It wasn't until later in the afternoon—after my swim, but with no particular concern that Mr. Taylor and I had not crossed paths—that I learned for whom the siren sounded. All of DOA.

Swim Date, There, There

I am sitting in the locker room. I have remembered my combination. I get up and go over to the fire extinguisher and get
Mr. Taylor's numbers. I open his locker. The white tape with its
marks is there. There is room for another row. I take down his
bowl of soaps: Lisbon. London. Mexico City. I imagine myself in
the third person doing theme kitchens: Toto is in the wallpaper.
I am a morning television doctor who comes on with the coffee
maker. I am talking but I can't quite make out what I am saying.

The camera backs up and reveals a girl in a black tank suit
sitting beside me. She is taking phone calls from the viewing
audience. My ISM wants to know what to take for the pain of
moderation. Someone who sounds very much like myself asks
about the effects of old athletic injuries on the life of the mind,
and what are the best prophylactics for the loss of memories.
Water, says a voice from somewhere. All of water everywhere.
Mr. Taylor calls to say that we have lived a long and useful life
by not going to Florida in the winter. The girl beside me makes
no comment as she goes from caller to caller, clicking them on
and off with the twist of a tiny button on the voice speaker. *All
of water*, I hear myself saying through the buzz of yet another
nerve dying.

I put back the bowl of soaps and place Mr. Taylor's combination inside his locker and shut the door and snap the lock. I go
over to my own locker, open it, and stand there for a moment
trying to see the near past. Nothing. No vision of laps done. I
am not at any base. No Flatbush Holy Land Bronx Kansas. No
irony. The line-up card is empty. There is nothing in my locker
but my tank suit, my goggles, a towel.

I walk into the lobby. I have patients this afternoon: stomach
discomfort that will need Raglan; we are beginning to see some

flu; young men from the College come in with condoloma. *There, there,* I will say to them all. *Have you thought about creeks and ox-bows? Would you like an irony? Take two with a bay of water and don't call me.*

There, there, we say to ourselves.

A lithe and lovely girl in a skirt and sweater carrying a bathing bag says hello as we pass each other on the sidewalk outside the pool.

THE SKULL HUNTER

I call myself the Skull Hunter, and I guess I am. It's not painted on the side of my pickup or anything. And the guy I work for doesn't have any name for my job, only, "My man Wallace will take care of you." I work for Karl Ganz who owns Whitewoman River Floats and Motel. Karl doesn't know anything about the skulls. Neither does his wife. She left him last year and is living in Denver. I mean to go see her some day when I'm out there. I think I will.

I have a wife and I have this woman on the river. Sally Norton is her name. I like to mess with women. I like my wife. We don't have any children. *Nothing in the oven*, my wife will say and pat her belly. We live at the motel. Number 26. It's one of the cabins. The biggest one. We get it as part of our pay. My wife cleans for the motel. And she makes extra money by fixing picnic baskets for the floats. Karl knows about the picnics, but he doesn't want a cut. I let my wife keep it for herself. She buys flowers or plants. Spring through the fall. She makes 26 a home. It's nice.

Sometimes she'll go to Cottonwood and buy clothes. Pretty clothes she wears for me at night. It's always good to come home to her, even if I've been with Sally Norton, or sometimes with another woman I have in Cottonwood. It will be the same if I ever get with Karl's wife in Denver. I'll be driving back at night having nailed Karl's wife but looking to see mine. You have to know how I feel to understand.

What I do when I'm not working the river is keep the motel fixed. Plastic pipe made plumbers of us all, and a cordless drill makes you a carpenter. I put doors right when they've pulled off their hinges. Fix windows. Screens. Steps. In the summer between floats I paint. Inside and out. The motel is yellow, but not inside. Inside is white. I change light bulbs. Before I was a pen rider in Ogallala.

"My man Wallace will come right down, lady, and change that light bulb pronto." *Pronto* is one of Karl's big words. We do everything pronto at the Whitewoman Floats and Motel. The lady who wanted her light bulb changed, that's another story. She and her husband are regulars. Every July. The story's not like you think. It's more fucked than that. My wife and I have never told anyone. Like I've not told Karl about the skulls.

The deal with the skulls is this. We have these canoes that Karl rents to float the Whitewoman starting with this one group that comes from Tulsa in wetsuits the end of March. Then the summer floaters. Then all the way through early October when we get people who want to see how the leaves have turned along the river. It's warm here mostly through Thanksgiving. Winter is something else. But I like that, too. Ice in the wind.

Karl's made this deal with the ranchers along the river to clean up any mess his floaters leave. That way Karl doesn't have the ranchers down on the river yelling at the floaters to stay off their land. The river's not theirs but the land is. My job is to go down the river when a float's over and pick up after them. That's when I hunt for my skulls. Then, and other times as well. I was the one that came up with the idea about the fences.

Every time the river runs from one ranch to another, there's a fence. Even across the water. Which means the floaters have to slip under the fence, and it's barbed wire. What Karl used to do, he'd give everybody a pair of cheap work gloves to push up the wire as they'd go under. Only they'd get scraped anyway. Along their arms. And once this lady from the Plaza, Kansas City, got her hairdo caught in the wire and started screaming like she was on fire. She jumped out of the canoe and wouldn't get back in. At least that's what they said when the rest of them got to the end of the run where I was to meet them up at the Two Sleeps Bridge and drive them back to the motel. They said she was just sitting on the bank about a mile up river and somebody'd have to get her by truck because she wasn't anymore getting into the canoe. Her husband said leave the bitch to walk out. The dizzy bitch.

After I drove everybody up the Oil Road to the motel, I went back to the Whitewoman and got her, only it wasn't easy because she was where Bone Creek comes in, and you can't get down to the river there by truck, so I had to walk the last part. That's when I thought about just cutting open a length of PVC pipe and slipping it over the bottom strand of wire so you could just hold it up with your hand when you took the canoe under. Even if it did drop down, it wouldn't get caught in your hair or anything.

I told my thinking to the Kansas City lady as we walked out, but she was still fucked from the fence getting caught in her hair, and I don't think she paid much attention. I liked her, though, and I took her hand a few times to pull her up banks. I opened the door to the truck and helped her in. If you're nice to women, they'll be nice to you. Maybe not right away, but sooner or later. Maybe it doesn't mean you'll nail them, but it's a start.

I think of things like that. I think that all women are related when it comes to how men treat them, so that the word gets around about you. Like the birds know when my wife starts filling up the feeders in the winter. Or animals will know where to find water in a dry year and tell one another. I've not worked the idea out all the way to the end, but that's the start of it. Ideas are like women because they're fun to think about when you're by yourself. On the river, I'm by myself a lot. Unless I'm with Sally Norton.

You can't see where Sally lives from where Bone Creek comes into the Whitewoman. Or even from where I had to park my truck to go down to get the lady from Kansas City. But where she lives is not far away. Up river two bends. Near where I found my first buffalo skull. And my third. Across from the oxbow nobody knows about. Or the dugout with this guy's skeleton on his back with no head on his shoulders. Near there. All around are good skull-hunting pastures. The best.

What I do is sell the skulls. The cattle skulls. Other skulls. But not the buffalo skulls. I don't sell those. I sell the cattle skulls in Denver to this guy who cleans them up for his shop. It's called the High Plains Hangout. I also sell him wild turkey feathers. Rattlesnake skins. Coon tails. Arrowheads. Mainly I sell him cattle skulls and deer skulls. Hawk skulls. Horse skulls. Coyote skulls. Two bobcats skulls, both from the same year. But mainly cattle skulls. It's my specialty.

Every time I go to Denver with a load of skulls, he takes me to the Buffalo Exchange for lunch. The place is full of animal heads on the walls. He treats me to a buffalo burger and some Fat Tire beer. That's a name, now isn't it? Fat Tire beer. I think he should get a better name for his store, but I don't say so. Maybe *Skull Heaven*. Something.

"Do you ever find any buffalo skulls?" he asks me the other day.

"No," I say.

"They say sometimes they'll wash out of the river banks in the spring," he says.

"That'd be the time," I say.

"If you ever find one, I'll pay top dollar for it," he says. He buys me another Fat Tire.

I don't tell him I have seven good buffalo skulls from the river. I don't tell anyone. Not even my wife. Nobody. Seven. Only Sally Norton knows about them because that's where I keep them. At her double-wide up from Bone Creek. Then there's plenty I don't tell Sally, either. Mostly, I don't tell her much. There's more to me than I've ever told anybody. Especially women.

"I mean top dollar," he says. "If it's old. From the Indian days. Not one of Ted Turner's buffalo. And not busted up."

"Sure," I say. I tell him I'll keep an eye out.

We go back to his shop, and he pays me for what I've brought, and I look around and see what I've sold him before that's still on the walls and tables, and what prices he gets for the cattle skulls after he's bleached them out in a tub of Clorox so they look like they've been in the pastures half of history. Some of them he's had painted. I wouldn't pay what you have to pay to own one of my skulls, but I'm glad somebody does.

Then I head home. Four hours. I like the drive because most of the time it's sunny out here, and in the afternoon coming back across the Front Range you get these long shadows from behind, filling in the creek beds and draws and canyons like it was dark snow, and I like that.

"Sell everything?" my wife says.

"Five hundred and twenty-seven dollars worth of everything," I say. She is dressed in this buckskin skirt and a red blouse with the top two buttons not done, and that means she wants some pleasure for herself. When she's like this, she doesn't like to wait until after supper. Karl says women always want to wait. They want some romance before they get nailed. Not my wife. Not tonight at least. She's got two beers in frosted mugs, and I can see her tits are trying to unbutton number three all by themselves. I take my pleasure; she takes hers. Afterward, we finish our mugs in bed.

"The man in cabin eighteen left me another note," she says when we're eating supper. To let me look at her across the table, she hasn't put her blouse back on. Only her buckskin skirt. That's to get me going a second time, and it might work. "It was under the pillow," she says.

The man in cabin eighteen is the husband of the woman who wanted me to change the light bulb a few years back, and that's when all this started. They're from Omaha. A pair of lawyers. Or something. Professional people is what they say for themselves. That's lawyers, we figure. Or college teachers.

"They're something," I say.

My wife has fixed meat loaf, and it's good. She puts egg in it and bread crumbs and onions and steak sauce on the top so she gets this deep-red crust. I can't have it any better. I drink my Coors out of the frosted mug she's fixed and look at my wife and think about my ride across the Front Range with $527 in the glove compartment all the time, coming home to her wanting to get nailed twice, and I say to myself I am one happy Skull Hunter. Maybe I should put that on the side of my truck. *One Happy Skull Hunter.*

"They want us tomorrow," she says. "After supper."

"Was there any money?" I say.

"Twenty bucks," my wife says. She points to it under a sunflower magnet she has on the refrigerator. It's one of those new twenty-dollar bills.

What cabin eighteen wants is for us to watch them while they do it. Sometimes it's enough they can see us at the back window looking through into the bedroom, but sometimes they want us in the living room. When they want us in the living room, they don't want us to watch, just listen. They are older than we are, but they can really go at it.

When they've asked, we've never not done it. It will be

the same this time. We always spend the twenty on something special. Dinner out in North Platte, usually. Or Cottonwood. There's a good Mexican place in Cottonwood. The woman I have in Cottonwood is a waitress there. We try not to look at each other. Only, sometimes we do. She's younger than me. By a lot. When I'm with her, I show her some things she doesn't know about. It's fun.

"City people are weird," says my wife, as she gets up to clear the table. I look at her naked back and to tell the truth her back and her shoulders and all the way down to where her skirt is tight across her waist is just as beautiful to me as anything else she's got for a body. Just as pretty going away half naked as coming at me. You can't like a woman better than that.

"City people are weird," she says again, as she turns toward me after having put the dishes on the counter.

"That they are," I say. "Any other notes?"
My wife gets these other notes when she's cleaning the rooms, from guys looking to nail her.

"One," she says as she sits down. "From six. No money, though. You want to read it?"

She saves the notes. She keeps them for a journal she's writing about how we live out here. Like the guy does in *Dances with Wolves*. It's her favorite movie. I can't watch it. Not what happens at the end to the horse. Or to the wolf. I can't even watch it as far as when they find the buffalo all skinned. I just can't.

My wife wants me to keep a journal, too. About the floats. The skulls. She says I can't use the notes she gets, even though she lets me read them. Some are just shit-house notes. Most guys don't know how to write women. Some are pretty smooth. I left her one, myself, but she doesn't know that. She said it was the best one she ever got, and I still haven't told her. Maybe I should. Maybe not. I've been trying to figure out what you should tell women. Even your wife.

"I'll read it later," I say, because if it's a shit-house note, then it will spoil it for me with her for a second time. If it's good, I'd rather have written it myself.

"You hunting skulls tomorrow?" my wife says, with a smile on her face and tossing her hair back because she knows she's going to get me again. Then she touches her breasts with her fingers and watches herself do it.

"Yes," I say. I need another ten minutes or so.

"You going to take me along," she says.

She's poking me. But just for fun this time. She knows I won't take her on the river. Or to Denver. It's a scab between us. I have this theory that a man's got to have his own territory. Some place where he's different from what he is when he's not there. Not that I'm not who I am when I'm with my wife. I'm me wherever I am. It's just that there is more than one me. Men are that way. Like my thinking about women, I haven't got it all lined out, but I'm working on it. Thinking takes time if you do it right.

"I'll take you some place else," I say. "Florida." I don't mean it.

"How about we do it on the river sometime?" she says back.

I can tell she's just thought of it. And it sounds good. We did it once on a mattress in the pickup at night in the high school parking lot. It was her idea.

"Turn the canoe over," she says, as she gets up from the table and walks toward the bedroom, bending a little at the waist as she goes.

"Maybe," I say. I mean it. Only I'll take it back later. "Yes," I say and follow her into the bedroom.

Like I say, it's when I take a canoe down the river to see if the floats have left anything, I hunt for cattle skulls. Sometimes they wash over the bank. Sometimes they are in the water or on the sandbars. Mainly they are in the pastures, which means I get off the river to find them. Or stop by Sally Norton's.

Her husband was a trapper. He's still alive even after he shot himself, but he can't make it on his own anymore, so he's in Cottonwood at the home for cripples. I'm the one who saved him. I think maybe Sally shot him. I can sort of see it. Sally's a little fucked. The bullet went through his neck. He's a lot older than she is, and some people say he never was her husband. I found him by one of his traps. He was out, but he wasn't bleeding as bad as you'd think. I put him in my canoe and took him down to the Two Sleep Bridge. Tom Bitters came by about then, and we laid out Sally's husband in the back of the truck and drove him into Cottonwood where they said he wasn't dead. I hadn't been with Sally before he got shot, but I was afterward. That night, if you want to know.

I hunt my cattle skulls between floats during the summer, but I also hunt them in the spring before the guys with the wetsuits from Tulsa come out. That's when I go down the river to cut the logs out of it so the floats can get through. I fix the fences, as well. It's cold in March, but I like it better for hunting skulls because I don't feel rushed. I also like going down the Whitewoman after the last float in the fall, even if it's November or December and we've got some snow. With a good snow blowing on the river, you can't believe anybody was ever on it before you were, no matter how many floaters came through in the summer. There's something clean about winter out here.

It's in the spring when you find the buffalo skulls. Just like the guy in Denver says. They come out of the banks after a good rain. You've got to know where to look. You've got to know what you're looking for, also. I do. I know.

I look for a dark lump in the clay of the bank. Or for bones coming out. Ribs. Legs. Backbones. The skull will be along there somewhere. I've been lucky. The seven buffalo skulls I've found have all been good. Both horns. No eye sockets broken in. Noses all the way to the end. Big skulls. From *Dances With Wolves* days. I wouldn't know what top dollar would be in Denver for my seven skulls. But they're not for sale.

When I found number seven last fall is when I found my skeleton. But not his head. I call him Wallace. After me. He's all there. Feet. Arms. Ribs. All connected. On his back. Everything but the head. I've been the year up and down the river looking for it. No head.

I leave Wallace where I found him because nobody would know to look there. I check in on him now and then. He's in a dugout in a small oxbow. There are mud cats in it. It's big enough for that. You can't see it from the river because of some plum thickets. I didn't know it was there myself until I came on it from walking the pasture behind it.

I don't think Wallace is old. Not like a buffalo skull will be old. But he's not young either. He's not like someone who came out on the river two years ago and got murdered or died and I need to tell the sheriff. Or somebody got left on a float like that guy from Kansas City wanted to leave his wife. Wallace has been around. I like to think that maybe he lived on the river and no one knew he was out here. A guy by himself. Who knows? I talk to him.

Sometimes, I imagine Wallace just packed it in one day from Chicago or Detroit during the Depression and found himself this oxbow and made his dugout and called it home. Other times, I think he was the last of the mountain men who wanted a place to live out his days where you can see the edge-of-the-earth morning, night and noon.

I got other ideas for him, as well. A hitchhiker from the

highway who maybe had robbed a bank in Missouri. Some guy from Hays who went out for a pack of cigarettes on his wife and kids. Maybe an old Indian who escaped from the reservation in Oklahoma and came up here to this oxbow to die. I think I'll name the oxbow Wallace's Oxbow. In honor of him, not me. Wallace's Oxbow it is. Why not?

Every time I stop by, I add to his story about how he lived on the river. He's fishing with a taut line in the summer and setting snares for rabbits in the winter. I've given him my Model 12 so he can shoot prairie chickens. I'm thinking I should give him my 250 Savage so he can take a deer. Tan out the hides. Maybe one of the old deer skulls that washed out of the river last spring is one he shot. I make his stories with stuff like that in them. Maybe Wallace had a horse. A dog. But not a wolf. I don't want him to have a wolf. I tell him he doesn't have a wolf.

When I finish talking to Wallace, I go over to Sally Norton's double-wide. Her husband hauled it in over the Cody ranch about ten years ago. It was rough when he brought it in, and it's worse now. The roof is held down by tires, and some of the siding is starting to flap off. If the wind's up, I can hear it creak from the river. You can't use one room at all because the windows are out. That's where I keep my buffalo skulls.

I've got them all laid out on a big blanket, three down each side, and the best one at the top. I call him Bill. When Sally's not around, like she wasn't the other afternoon, and I'm waiting for her, I'll go into the room and lie down on my back so that the skulls are up my sides with Bill above my head. I like doing that. I like doing that and waiting for Sally and thinking about the way she likes to get nailed.

"I know where it is," Sally Norton says to me.

We're done and she's starting to come down. Right afterward she can't talk. She's pretty, but not as pretty as my wife. She makes different noises though. All along, she doesn't talk no matter how we go at it. But she makes these noises. First one kind of noise then another. Then at the end, all the noises at once. Like a lot of animals at once. After that is when she can't talk. You nail different women for different reasons.

"What?" I say. I pretend I don't know what she's talking about. But I do. The thing is, I didn't know she knew about Wallace. I never told her. Because she lives on the river, she might know about the oxbow but not the dugout. You don't know it's there.

"The head," she says.

"What head?" I say.

"I have it," she says.

"Where?"

"I'm not going to tell you."

I'm late getting home, and my wife has dinner on the table and she's got the candles lit, and she's been to Cottonwood to buy some new clothes with the money she's been saving up from the picnics, plus the forty bucks we got for watching the lawyers do it twice this summer.

She's wearing a yellow blouse with nothing on underneath. I'm not sure if I've got enough stuff left over from this afternoon, but I think if I can put her off until after dinner maybe I do. I've done it before back to back. It helps when the women are different. But I'm getting older. I can feel it.

"Let's eat first," I say as I sit down. "I've got a story to tell you." I don't, but my wife likes my stories and this might slow her down, although I can see she's breathing like she wants to do it yesterday, and that makes her tits shiver and I worry that they'll unbutton her new blouse from the inside out.

"What's your story?" she says. She's still standing, and I can see that she's bought this new skirt as well. It's yellow, too, only not so yellow as her blouse. I can see her legs through it. When she notices that I'm looking, she backs up some so I can get a better view. I'm in a tough spot here.

"Sit down and I'll tell you," I say.

"It better be good," she says, bringing a plate of baked chicken with her from the stove, and some corn and bread and potatoes as well. Two frosted beers.

I am trying to think of a story about some adventure I've had on the river or in Denver that she knows isn't true because it couldn't be. Like the story I once told her about sitting next to Jane Fonda in the Buffalo Exchange and how we talked about Fat Tire beer and buffalo burgers. My wife asked if Jane Fonda showed me some of her exercises that are on this videotape my wife has, and I say yes, she did. Then I say I did situps with Jane Fonda right there on the floor in the Buffalo Exchange with the skull buyer and everybody watching and clapping. Then Ted Turner comes in. My wife said Ted and Jane have split, and so he wouldn't be there. But I say he is. That kind of story.

Or maybe I could go on with my white horse story. We've got this white horse out here that we like to think is wild. Some people have seen him and some have not. I've seen him, but not up close. On a ridge. Or down in Black's Canyon. On the river way up in front of me. He's around. Once at Bone Creek, just about where I parked the pickup to get the lady from Kansas City. You make the sign of the white horse when you see him. Or even when you talk about him. That's for good luck.

Anyway, I have this story I tell my wife about the white horse, which I make up as I go along. One story at a time. About how we are friends because he comes down to the Whitewoman to drink and doesn't spook when he sees me, because he knows I'm on the river like he is. How I talk to him. What he does. How he lays his ears back. Then forward. I put myself in his mind and have him think about me. He knows me, I tell my wife. He whinnies, seeing me in the canoe. Snorts low. Paws the ground. Rearing as if he's happy to see me. In my white horse stories, I haven't touched him yet. I thought I'd do that later. But I have him all white, although most everybody who has seen him says there's a bit of a gray blanket on his rump.

But with my wife sitting across from me in her new yellow blouse and this red ribbon in her black hair, I can't think of any stories like the ones from Denver or about the white horse because I hadn't set my mind to do it. After you've nailed a woman, the stories just go out of you. Not that I tell Sally Norton my stories. Or any other woman I'm with. Only my wife gets my stories. Just now, I'm a dry creek bed. So then I think maybe I should tell my wife the truth about something. Something she doesn't know.

"I found a buffalo skull," I say.

"No," she says. She knows I've been looking for one. She knows the man in Denver said he'd pay us good money for one. If good money is $500, she wants to go to Kansas City and stay on the Plaza when they've got the Christmas lights up.

"Yes," I say.

"Where?" she says. "Is it in the truck? Can I see it?" She knows this isn't a story I've made up. Right away she knows that.

"In Dull Knife's Cut by Bone Creek," I say. "On the south side." I don't know why I'm saying this. It's not good. I can feel something bad coming.

"Is it in the truck?" she says again. She's drained her beer so she gets up for another one and brings me one as well. I don't want to look at her because she's got nothing on but her new blouse and skirt, and I'm not ready yet. I don't say anything for a moment, and she asks again if it's in the truck, and she is about to go get it if I say yes. I hear myself say:

"I left it at Sally Norton's double-wide."

My wife drills me. She puts the mug down real slow. It doesn't even make a noise when it hits the table. She's still drilling me. Outside I think I can hear Ganz start his pickup. Maybe not. Maybe one of the cabins.

"I'll cut her gut button out with my Queen Steel," my wife says. "And shove it down her throat."

Sometimes in the early fall, you get these really warm nights with a moon to them. It's a good time to go down the river, and so I do. I'm not looking to go back to Sally's. I won't float that far. Just to the grain train bridge, then pull out and walk myself home. It's only about an hour's ride down, and if I cut across Lakin's pasture instead of taking the tracks, it's only twenty minutes. Maybe by then it will be better. I put the canoe in the bed of the pickup and go.

What I like to do on the river at night is mainly think. It's a pleasure to itself. Just like going down in the day time looking for skulls is a pleasure. Only thinking is different from looking for skulls, and I do it best at night, even off the river. In bed with my wife twitching in her dreams beside me. Or sometimes coming back over the front range at night after I've been to Denver. I talk to myself, but not out loud. I keep it all in my head. You don't waste it that way.

What I'm thinking as I go down the river is about all the things I could have told my wife that are true that I haven't told her. That I've only told Wallace. About how I was married once before in Ogallala where I was a pen rider. Or how I was in the Navy just out of high school and that I might be wanted because I don't know how many years have to go by on an AWOL not to get busted. Or about my mother and how she died because of me. How I once was with Ganz's wife. But only once. Not that I wouldn't do it again if I could find her in Denver. Which maybe I can. Or about Wallace.

When his wife left him, Ganz told me that women have the most secrets, but I don't know. I am going down the river with the moon coming up in front of me, and I am thinking of all the stories about me I have kept secret from my wife. I am thinking that they are the stories I wouldn't want anyone to know but her. But I haven't told her any of them. Only bullshit stories about the white horse and Jane Fonda. Who wants to go belly up full of true stories he hasn't told anybody but a skeleton with no head in a dugout? I think that's what happened to Wallace. No stories for himself but the ones I make up for him. Not for me, I think. I have my wife. I can tell my wife everything. I have enough stories for her to last until we're dead

I think what I should do is tell my wife something true once a week. On Fridays. Plus special days when we go out for dinner after the couple in cabin 18 have given us twenty bucks. Just take the heat from her until she gets used to it. Maybe I'll mix up my stories to start with. Tell her one of my Denver stories or something from the river. Then tell her one on me that's true. Not to fool her. Just to mix them up as if what's true about me is no different than what's not. I'll do it, I think. It's a plan. I'll go there. I feel good about it.

But coming around a bend in the river and out from under the bluffs, I think it's a bad plan. There's a lot of trouble waiting for you in the truth of things. At least with me there might be. What's the point? She'll get over Sally Norton. I've been caught before. Why set my own trap then step in it? Every Friday for a lifetime. Maybe I'll cut a deal whereby I won't see Sally anymore. Maybe drop the woman in Cottonwood, even though my wife doesn't know about her. Just find a woman in Denver because that's over the edge of the earth and news doesn't travel back across. Life is as good as it's going to get if I can smooth out my wife. Trying to make it perfect will just fuck it up. Then I see him. The white horse.

He's standing under this ash tree that dropped a big limb into the water last winter that I had to cut up and haul away so the floaters wouldn't have to get out of their canoes. He's standing right there. Because the wind's against me, he doesn't know I'm on the river. I break paddle and ease the canoe onto a small bar. It doesn't crunch. He's still standing there. This is no story. I can see him just like I've said I could. He lays his ears forward, then they go up. Then back. He's got no blanket. He's all white, like I tell it. I can see he's been to water. I can see the hoof prints in the sand where he's been. I'm that close. I can see his eyes. Black, like I make them. I wait for him to give me that low rumble I tell he has. He doesn't. His ears go up. He's thinking how the river is his every night. He's thinking about me and Wallace's Oxbow, and even Wallace, because he's been at the dugout, too. Which is true because I've seen his hoof prints. *I was Wallace's horse, I have him think. When Wallace went belly up, I went wild. I know where Sally Norton put his head. And where it was before she found it. I know about the skulls, and when I go belly up I want the Skull Hunter to have my head. But only for himself. Not to go to Denver. Only for himself. And his wife.*

Then he bolts. Not down stream but straight at me because he's heard something behind him. He bolts right up the river bed, and in maybe three strides he's in my face. Then over the front of the canoe so close I get splattered with water and sand. I'd like to think he saw me, that we locked eyes and all that, but to tell the truth, I don't think he did. Only the canoe, which he probably took to be a log.

I can't turn around fast enough to see him leave the river, so I don't know if he went up the north bank or the south. He just wasn't there. Not even the sound of him going away was there. Only the breeze in the ash tree and water. Water coming around the bend and lapping against the canoe. Then I hear it. Something coming up the river. Deer, I think. It's in the middle of the river, whatever it is. Then I hear it talking to itself, and it's Sally Norton. The way the river lays right here, and because I'm in the dark of the bank under the ash tree, I can see her but she can't see me. Just like with the white horse.

She's walking along in her bare feet. I can see her that clear. It's a little late in the year for wading in the Whitewoman, but Sally's tough. She's naked like when I left her that afternoon. I see her tits in the moonlight. They're not as nice as my wife's tits, but they're nice. I'm going to tell my wife that. How her tits are better than Sally's. Maybe not. It's true, though. Sally's carrying my skull. She's got Wallace. In her right hand. Fingers in the eye holes. Swinging it as she walks. Just talking to herself about what I don't know.

Looking at her with Wallace's head in her hand, I don't think about Sally. Not even about how I nailed her earlier. Not about the noises she made or any of it. I couldn't get into my mind if I wanted to, and I'm not thinking of my wife that way, either. I'm not thinking about my wife. I'm not thinking about her yellow blouse. Although I could. I know I could. I'm thinking again about what I'm going to tell her when I get back if she's still there and hasn't gone down to Sharon Springs to stay with her brother and his wife. I hope not, because I've changed my mind again. I'm thinking, seeing the white horse is where I'm going to start with what's for real and what's not.

When I think that, then I start thinking about my wife in all kinds of ways with her tits moving under her yellow blouse and her legs and how good it is to nail her, and I can feel my trouser trout swimming in my pants. It's not just about nailing her. It's about how I'm going to take her down the Whitewoman, even now, late as it is, and show her where I found every one of the buffalo skulls. I'll get them out of Sally Norton's double-wide, and when my wife and I go down the river I'll put them back where I found them just so she can see. Maybe even hide one beforehand and pretend like she's the one who found it. I'll show her Wallace's Oxbow. I'll show her Wallace. I'll tell what I've made up about Wallace and let her pick the story about him she likes the best. After that we'll turn the canoe over like she wants to. And I'll nail her on the river. Then we'll go look for cattle skulls in the pastures together, and when we find enough I'll take her with me to Denver and I'll do sit-ups for her in the Buffalo Exchange and we'll have ourselves a Fat Tire beer. I'll ask the bartender if Jane Fonda's been in recently. I'll introduce her to Ted Turner when he shows up. *This is my One Happy Skull Hunter wife,* I'll say to Ted Turner. *Jane and me have made up,* he'll say.

I'm thinking all this as I'm looking at Sally Norton coming up the Whitewoman with my skull in her right hand, and then she's gone. Not there. Maybe I looked away for a moment like you do when you're thinking about something. I don't remember. I just know Sally's gone. Tits and skull and bare feet and talking and all.

There's nothing on the river but me. Me and everything that's inside me for having been out here. Now and before. Summer and winter. Floats. Seeing the lump of a buffalo skull coming out of the bank. Cattle skulls in the pastures. Looking for Wallace. Talking to him in his dugout. That woman from Kansas City. More. It's all in me. Sally Norton. The white horse. It's all me. I've filled up the river with me.

Then I feel myself going home to see my wife. It feels good. Not that I know what I'll tell her.

NOTES ON THE COLD WAR IN KANSAS

Russian Radiation

There were three of us who were friends in those days when I was a young boy and lived in a small town in Kansas: Benny and Than (short, I suppose, for Nathan). We were all members—the only members—of The Society of the Secret Shed.

It was the 1950s, and one winter, Grandmother White caught me putting snowballs in the basement freezer to use the following year for a summer snowball war. I say Grandmother White "caught me" because she was sure that the snows in Kansas—and all across America—were laced with "Russian radiation." Grandmother White was my father's mother.

"We'll have to throw it all out," said Grandmother White. She meant the food in the freezer: half a steer bought from—and butchered by—a local rancher. Some sausage from a farm pig. Bacon as well. Two catfish from Wagnall's pond I had caught that fall and was proud to have done so. Vegetables and strawberries from our garden that we had picked and frozen the previous summer. Whole chickens we bought live from the Simms' down the road. It was Grandmother White who had slaughtered the chickens, chopping off their heads with my father's hatchet and then hanging them by one foot from the clothesline, using her collection of string. It was my job to catch the chickens as they flopped and ran—however briefly—headless around our back yard.

"I don't know," my mother said, looking into the freezer. "It seems such a waste." When my father got home from work, he made the decision: the food stayed.

"Your son will glow in the dark and parts of him will not be useful," said Grandmother White. "The rest of us will get tumors before our time. And warts too thick for a found penny to rub away. I know about the Russians." Grandmother White's real name, I later learned, was Grandmother Wakowski.

The snowballs could go, said my father. But the food stayed. He winked at me to say we'll find someplace else for the snowballs. Which we did.

"Parts of him will not be useful," said Grandmother White, glancing at me. I thought she meant my throwing arm and that I would lose at summer snowball war—or worse, that I would be unable to play baseball in the local Three-Two League. I held my right arm with my left hand. My father patted me on the back. We stored the snowballs in Uncle Bert's freezer. "Don't tell your grandmother," my father had said.

The Girl Next Door

Sharon Fulton (for some reason I always thought of her by her full name, never just Sharon, or even Sherry—which is what her mother, and mine, called her) went to the Catholic school (Bishop Something or Other), while I attended Hickory Grove, the public school. I did this over the protests of Grandmother White, who might have changed her name but not her religion. Hickory Grove was a brief bike ride away from where we lived; Sharon Fulton's school was on the far north side of town.

Sharon Fulton's bus picked her up fifteen minutes before I had to leave for Hickory Grove, so as I got ready in the mornings, I could see her standing at the end of her driveway. Yellow became my favorite color because it seemed to be her favorite color: yellow blouses when school started and then again in late spring; yellow sweaters in fall; a yellow and black winter coat; yellow dresses that blossomed with the fifties foliage of petticoats and in which Sharon Fulton would, while waiting for her bus, twist her hips this way and that, as if to get them to settle. It was because of Sharon Fulton that I was always on time for school. It is also true that until the day I dug the atomic bomb fallout shelter, Sharon Fulton and I never spoke. And after that we never spoke.

Binoculars

Than's father had a pair of binoculars. Navy beer bottles, he called them. From Than's house I could read our name on our mailbox. I could see to the bottom of the lot and the line of small trees that hid The Secret Shed. If you stood on a chair, you could spot the flagpole on our school, even if the flag wasn't up.

"Let me see. My turn," is what the three of us would say as we passed around the binoculars. Once, I saw Sharon Fulton standing in her front yard. "That's enough," Than's father said just at that moment. He had been in the war (as had my father), and I suppose he wanted to be careful about his souvenirs from those days. "That's enough," and Sharon Fulton vanished.

Civil Defense

Than and Benny and I were Boy Scouts. For a merit badge, we needed to perform some kind of public service.

"I think we should clean up Turkey Creek," said Than one day at the shed. "It's full of bottles, and cans, and trash. We could use my uncle's pickup." Than was always trying to figure out how to make use of, or ride in, (front or back—but the back was preferred) his uncle's pickup. "It's got a winch on it," said Than, as if that were the clincher. He cranked an imaginary handle.

For Benny's part, he was always plotting ways to use his .22—a bolt-action single-shot rifle that had been provisionally given to him the previous Christmas, and which could only be used with his grandfather present, and then only for target practice on tin cans. Benny's father had been killed in Germany.

"I think we should shoot the pigeons at the Co-Op," said Benny. "My mother says they're a menace." Benny aimed a long stick and fired off a few shots at some starlings on the power line that ran above the shed. "Dead menace. Bang. Dead menace. Bang." "Menace" was a new word for Benny.

"I think we should join the Civil Defense," I said. "That way we could get binoculars to look for Russian bombers." I held up two rounded fists to my eyes and turned my head this way and that, scanning the Kansas sky for enemy planes. The dream of binoculars to look for Russian atomic bombers beat out the pickup truck and the pigeon menace.

The Secret Shed

It was an old chicken house located on a bank above a small nameless (and mostly dry) creek that ran into Wagnall's pond. Overgrown with morning glory vines and ringed with a barricade of sunflowers and thistle, it was hidden (so we thought) from everyone but the three of us. The Shed had board floors, under which the three of us stashed various odds and ends (totems Than called them) that we would get out when we gathered for the meetings of The Society of the Secret Shed.

It was at these meetings that we decided what we would do for the rest of the day: snake hunting was always on the list; tree climbing usually; skating if Wagnall's pond was frozen, stone skipping if it was not; snowball war, winter or summer. Just as important, we planned what we would do the following week, month, and year.

This list included floating down the Smoky Hill River to the Kansas River on a raft, and then to New Orleans by way of Chicago. As the only fisherman among us, I would be responsible for catching fish. Benny would shoot squirrels and rabbits and birds with his .22; and because he liked to build fires—he built the one that finally burnt down the Secret Shed—Than said he would cook.

Our plans also included taking turns walking and riding double on Dan (an appaloosa that Benny's grandfather owned) to Montana to see Niagara Falls, then taking the A Train to New York City. However, our best trip was hitchhiking to Kansas City and 12th and Vine to see a "burr-lee-q" show. (This latter adventure was something Benny's brother, Leroy, had already done—hitchhiking and all). But, whatever our agenda, we never began a meeting of The Society of the Secret Shed without putting our totems on the two-by-fours that ran along the walls of the shed, each of us claiming a wall that was not used by the door.

Than had a bird's head skeleton, a horseshoe (that I coveted), plus a pretty nasty-looking rabbit skin that had been pried off the asphalt road that we took to Hickory Grove. He also had a collection of various animal bones—part of a jaw, some vertebra, what might have been a leg bone, ribs—that he was trying to assemble into a composite animal on the floor of The Shed, and over which we would have to step as we moved around.

As for Benny, he had a flattened quarter that had been crushed by the local grain train after we put it on the tracks; a spent CO_2 cartridge he said we could use to make a bomb by filling it with gun powder and attaching a firecracker fuse;

and two live .50 caliber machine gun rounds that his uncle had brought back from the war. Benny also claimed he was going to bring down some "Mexican" playing cards of his brother's with pictures of naked women on them—but he never did.

My totems were a greenish stone I found in a large catfish I had caught and cleaned. I would also put out a Lazy Ike lure, whose treble hooks I had straightened with a pair of pliers so I could claim—which I did—that a huge bass named Godzilla had struck the bait with such force he flattened the hooks.

But my prize totem—prized by all of us—was a page I had ripped out of a paperback book that had been in the rack of the local drug store. The page (page 126) had the words brassiere and breasts toward the bottom. The complete sentence ran: "When Tricia turned around, George saw that she had unbuttoned her blouse so that he could see her black brassiere and the tops of her white breasts." The following sentence was the fragment: "Then Tricia took off her blouse and reached behind her and un-" which broke off at the gully between page 126 and 127 (a page none of us had the nerve to return to the drugstore to steal).

At more than one meeting of The Society of the Secret Shed, we decided to find Tricia—or a Tricia—and invite her to join us on our trip to New Orleans. We were also inspired to name the raft for her: The Tricia. Our hope was that a real Tricia could go from page 126 to page 127 as we drifted toward Chicago by way of 12th and Vine streets in Kansas City. In the meantime, we had memorized her sentence-and-a half with the same fidelity we had memorized the Pledge of Allegiance we recited each morning at Hickory Grove Grade School.

Beyond our totems, it was required by The Society of the Secret Shed that each of us have a secret, secret, secret (being three, we thought of three as a sacred number) totem that was stored somewhere deep in The Shed. Both the location of this

Triple Secret Totem, and the object, itself, were not to be revealed to anyone, thus Benny had something somewhere, and so did Than—and I did not know what or where.

For my part (and I have kept my secret all these years), I had hidden in a crevice in a beam above the door a letter I was in the process of writing to Sharon Fulton, its opening sentence being: "I like yellow to" [sic]. Even then I needed an editor.

Physicals

"Yes," I am saying over the phone. "There are three of us, and we all want to join the Civil Defense. For our Boy Scout merit badge."

"Good for you," says the man at the other end. I cannot now recall by what means I tracked down whomever I am talking to, but somehow I had found my way to a pleasant and, as it will soon turn out, patient man. "What would you and your friends like to do for the Civil Defense?"

"We want to be spotters," I say.

"Spotters?"

"Yes," I say. "We want to look for Russian atomic bombers."

There are moments in everybody's youth when they know they are being fools. You don't know exactly why—or even for sure what it is to be a fool—but by some means you leap into your future, and you know that when you look back you will see yourself as very silly. In spite of this awareness, I go on.

"We want to look for Russian atomic bombers with binoculars. We would take turns during the school week. But in summer and on weekends we would all look. We each want our own pair."

"With binoculars?" says the man.

"Yes," I say.

"I see."

"We can climb trees," I say. "And we have a tree that gets us up to the roof of The Shed, so we have a good view from there." There is a pause.

"Do you know about physicals?" he says.

In point of fact, he had asked me if I knew about "physics"—not "physicals." Probably he was about to explain that whatever Russian atomic bomb was going to be dropped on The Shed (not to mention the Hickory Grove Grade School) would have been cut loose from the Russian atomic bomber somewhere around Denver, so that no matter how high a tree we climbed, no matter how powerful were our binoculars, or how diligent our looking through them from the roof of The Shed, we would not be able to see the Russian atomic bomb until it became its mushroom cloud.

However, for me, in hot pursuit of three pairs of binoculars and all the fame that would come with them, it made perfect sense that you would need physicals in order to be in the Civil Defense and issued Civil Defense binoculars. You had to have a physical to play in the Three-Two League, didn't you? There might even be a training program to get into the Civil Defense. If we had to take Civil Defense physicals, that might mean a day off from school, complete with the kind of excuse young boys dream of: I won't be in class on Friday, Miss Anderson, because I have to take a Civil Defense physical.

I saw myself returning to school with my binoculars hanging around my neck. "Navy beer bottles we call them," I would say to anyone who asked. I might even be required to stand at the classroom window—instead of taking my regular seat—all the better to scan the sky. At recess, the three of us would be "posted" around the playground looking Westward. (We always assumed the Russians would come from Colorado or California.) And finally in this movie I am making in my mind,

I am sure no one at Hickory Grove Grade School (not even Miss Anderson) would be allowed to talk to us when we were on duty.

Then there was Sharon Fulton. Someone would be assigned to look out for the Catholic girls at Bishop Whatever It Was. Someone would have to patrol the outer fence of the playground with binoculars scanning the sky. Someone would have to yell: Russian atomic bombers! Take cover! Under your desks! Russian atomic bombers! Sharon Fulton would faint. Someone would have to carry Sharon Fulton off the playground in her yellow dress. That someone would be me.

"We'll take physicals," I say.

Pubic Hair

It was Leroy, Benny's older brother, who first grew pubic hair. We even knew to call it "pubic hair" because you learned about it in Boys' Health, taught by the high school basketball coach, a Mr. Allen, who Leroy said was "doing the do" with Miss Anderson. Leroy was a hood.

Not that Leroy showed us his pubic hair; it was just that Benny reported on it from time to time. Benny's brother also shaved, had a switchblade knife, and kept a rubber in his wallet. (He did show us the rubber one day when Than and I stopped by). Later Leroy would get Roberta Taylor "hot"—whatever that meant. (What it finally meant was that Roberta Taylor got pregnant and was shipped off to Sharon Springs to her grandmother's farm.)

Leroy's pubic hair made us wonder about girls, and what, in Than's terminology, was "down there?" We couldn't really imagine what was "down there," this being well before *Playboy* showed us anything but breasts and buttocks—and in those days young boys in rural Kansas did not often get a hold of *Playboy*, so even breasts and buttocks were scarce items.

"I wonder if girls have pubic hair," Benny said one day at The Shed. Nobody said anything for a moment. For my part, I was hoping our meeting would be short, as in my mind I had composed two more sentences of my serial letter to Sharon Fulton, a letter I would only take out when Than and Benny had left.

"Girls do not have pubic hair," I pronounced.

"How do you know?" said both Than and Benny.

"Because only boys have pubic hair," I said. "That is why it's in Boys' Health."

"Stern says his sister will take down her pants for a dollar," said Than. Stern was Leroy's age. He, too, was a hood, and Stern was his last name, not his first, which made him even more of a hood than Leroy. Stern's sister was our age. We had heard this before about her. But a dollar was a lot of money for us, as we got a quarter a week allowance (Benny probably got less) and could only put together another dollar or so by doing extra chores. Then there was the question of who would ask Stern's sister.

"I think girls do have pubic hair," said Benny.

"They can't have pubic hair," I said, "because they don't have beards."

"Why wouldn't they have pubic hair in Girls' Health just like we have pubic hair in Boys' Health?" said Benny.

"They have breasts instead," I said. "We don't have breasts in Boys' Health. We have pubic hair. So it's even-steven." To this day I love reasoning from limited available evidence.

"Do you think girls have pubic hair?" Benny asked Than. Than thought a moment. It seemed a long time. I was beginning to lose track of the two sentences I was going to write to Sharon Fulton.

"I think," said Than finally, "that girls have pubic hair, but that they shed it in the summer." It seemed right.

"I agree with Than," said Benny.

"So do I," I said. Meeting over.

After we left, I doubled back and got out my letter to Sharon Fulton and wrote my two sentences and then went home, happy in the knowledge that someday, somehow, she would find it—maybe in the rubble of nuclear destruction.

It would be later that summer that the three of us would get a dollar together and draw straws to see who would ask Stern's sister to take down her pants (Benny lost). When she finally did it, standing in a small clearing up hill from The Shed while the three of us sat on the peak of the roof, we were not really able to see what we saw—or tell anyone what we had seen. However, we all agreed she did not have pubic hair.

"I told you," I said.

"It's still summer," said Than. "They don't grow it back until Thanksgiving."

Grandmother White, Television, Warts, and the Reading of Codes

We didn't have a television and neither did Benny or Than. Than's uncle in Kansas City had a television, and he told Than that you could see *The Lone Ranger* on it. This did not seem possible to us.

"He comes right into the living room. Tonto, too," said Than.

"What about Silver?" asked Benny.

"Silver, too," said Than. "You just turn on the television and the Lone Ranger and Tonto and Silver all ride around. And talk. Just like on radio, only they're in your living room."

"I don't believe it," I said. But I did. I imagined Silver and Tonto and the Lone Ranger all projected into our house, riding along while canyons and rivers and bandits and hostile Indians appeared in front of the divan or by the kitchen door or in the hallway that lead to my bedroom—all as the plot required. How this happened, I wasn't sure, but I was sure I wanted it to happen in our house.

"Who's going to clean up the mess?" said Grandmother White. We were at supper, and I had asked if I might have a television for my "big" Christmas present, even though Christmas was months away.

"I don't think we can get television out here," my father said. "You have to be near a city."

"What mess?" said my mother. She was as alert to household untidiness as was Grandmother White.

"From all those cowboys and Indians traipsing through the house," said Grandmother White. "You heard the boy. That whole Ranger gang he listens to on the radio comes out of the television and into the living room. We don't need that."

"I don't think that's the way it works," said my father. "I think they are all on a screen like at a movie theater."

I was greatly disappointed to hear this, as my father was usually right about such things. But maybe not always.

"I'll clean up the mess," I said. "It can be one of my chores."

"We can talk about it later," said my mother. That meant that we would not talk about it later. If she had said, "I'll talk to your father," that meant, "I'll fix it with your father," just as my father's wink meant he'd fix it with my mother by hiding my snowballs in Uncle Bert's freezer. In such ways do children learn to read codes.

All of this talk in code may have diverted my grandmother's attention from *The Lone Ranger*, but it did not divert her attention from a wart that had recently come up on my index finger, and which she saw as irrefutable evidence of the spread of Russian radiation.

"I have a found penny," she said, "and we have a dish rag."

"Mother," said my father. That meant stop with this superstitious nonsense.

"Not that it will do much good," said my grandmother.

"Parts of him may already not be useful."

"Grandmother White!" said my mother in some alarm.

Grandmother White was quiet for a moment, and then under the table I could feel her foot tap mine. That meant if I'd let her rub my wart with her found penny so she could wrap the penny in the dish rag and bury it, she'd give me a quarter; it would turn out to be the quarter I'd contribute to have Stern's sister take down her pants.

Benny

Sometime during high school, Benny went to the Army. He was sent there by the local judge who said it was either the Army or jail. Or reform school. Benny had begun blowing up mailboxes with cherry bombs; then he blew up a toilet in high school with a CO2 cartridge filled with gun powder; then he stuffed a potato into the exhaust pipe of the local patrol car; then he ripped a rubber machine off the men's room of the Texaco station; finally, he started shoplifting. (He was caught stealing boxes of Russell Stover candy from the drugstore where I had stolen Tricia's page 126.) In the Army, he was first stationed in Korea; then he went to Vietnam. While I was taking graduate courses at the university, and Than was finishing his degree to be the veterinarian he is today, Benny was fighting in the Tet Offensive. Where he was killed: A fact I have only recently learned.

The Bomb Shelter and Sharon Fulton

Not long after Stern's sister had taken down her pants, I was digging a hole near The Shed to bury a bird I killed with my slingshot, and Sharon Fulton came up. I am to become a man who will never know what to do or say when first in the presence of women I find attractive. I once told a woman who had put on a stylish pea coat over her rather ample upper body, "My, what big buttons you have." What I said to Sharon Fulton was: "I'm digging a fallout shelter." It seemed like the thing to say to a girl whom I had saved a number of times by spotting Russian atomic bombers with my binoculars—not to mention carrying her to safety from the playground after she had fainted.

I suppose Sharon Fulton stood there for a moment and watched me. I hoped she hadn't noticed the dead bird. I did not look up.

"Why?" she said. It would turn out to be the only word Sharon Fulton ever said to me. I looked up. She was wearing yellow. I went back to digging.

"Because there are Russian atomic bombers coming," I said.

"Why?" she said. I stopped digging. I stood by the pile of dirt I had made. I put my foot on the dead bird. I remember thinking I had not imagined Sharon Fulton's voice.

"They are slow bombers," I said. I struck a pose by leaning on my shovel. Again, she asked why.

"Because they are very heavy," I said. "They have all this steel plate, and our fighters can't shoot them down because the bullets bounce off. We've been shooting at them for a week now, and nothing happens. They are over Hawaii and pretty soon they'll be over Guam." I made the rat-tat-tat sound of the .50 caliber machine-gun fire I supposed would come from the front end of an F-86 fighter. I did this with a series of finger jabs meant to convey the bullets themselves, but which caused me to drop my shovel and shift my foot off the dead bird.

Sharon Fulton looked at the sky. She looked east, toward her school and mine. There was nothing but clear Kansas sky all the way to Kansas City.

"They are coming from the west," I said, and, after picking

up my shovel, pointed toward our houses up the hill. "When they get here, they will black out the entire horizon. That's why you need an atomic bomb shelter. Otherwise when the radiation spreads, parts of us will become useless."

Sharon Fulton was crying. I am about to become a man who does not know what do when women cry.

"You can't come into my atomic bomb shelter if you cry," I said. Sharon Fulton turned her back on me and walked away.

"Stern's sister took her pants down," I said. "For a dollar."

Sharon Fulton began running up the hill toward home, all yellow and lovely in my mind to this day.

At supper, my mother wanted to know if something was the matter. Grandmother White said she hoped I hadn't tried to dig up the wash cloth with the found penny in it, because I'd get covered with warts just from touching it.

"Mother!" said my father. Here, he winked at me. As I didn't wink back, he said, "What's the matter, son?" I didn't know what to say.

And still don't.

Unless it is something to Sharon Fulton after all these years, and across what miles that separate us, I do not know: Yellow is still my favorite color. Even today, I don't know what to say to women who are to me now what you were to me then. I hear the sound of your voice. And the sound of your crying. If only you had fainted, I would have known what to do. My mother could never understand why I started being late for school. When Than burned down The Shed that winter, my letter to you went up in flames, but I remember every word of it—including the final sentence I added after you left me alone with my bomb shelter. It is code for all that I have written above, which I am now tapping out to you. Wherever you are. Whoever we have become.

Where I Am Now

We Are a Country of Stories

The sheep have been through the hay meadows in recent weeks. Dominique and his herders drive them in a round robin route of about twenty kilometers, staying two or three days in each meadow. My guess is there are three hundred, including goats. They were below me for two days, the ewes giving birth so that the lambs are growing the flock as it moves. Now they are west of me, past the village of St. Phillipe; I see them on my way to the Monday market in Castillon.

I live in a small stone house perched high in a vineyard. From my bedroom window, at a distance I see the castle of Montaigne. It is more than sufficiently large for royalty. Close by, and out the same window, is the wreck of Château Montagne, lived in by a *très difficile* countess who had her fingers broken (one at a time, according to the story going up and down the *côte*) last year by robbers until she produced the keys to her safe. Montaigne would not have believed it had he seen it himself. We are a country of stories. And skeptics.

I type in the mornings unless it is a market day, when I do my shopping. Food is dear, but wine is inexpensive—at least for the *vin en vrac* I buy from Monsieur R., stopping by his *chai* to fill my four-liter, straw-covered bottle and gossip in my weak French.

Afternoons I cut logs, clear brush, and help with the sheep at a small farm down the road. In exchange, I am offered meals and wood for my stove. I walk to work, as it is only five kilometers. I move my feet to move my words.

I may become a father: the farm had six of its sheep killed by a mad dog. One of the ewes had just given birth, and we saved the lamb (now named Molly). Because I carried her into the house and laid her by the fire bright, she thinks I am her mother and follows me everywhere, bleating, bleating for her bottle. I don't have a place for her, but I might rig one. We'll see.

The hunters are busy these days, shooting from early in the morning until sunset: pheasants, palombes (a dove-like bird that migrates through on its way to Africa), wild pigs, and small deer with a high-pitched bark. I see these men by the sides of the small roads that wind through the hills, sometimes with dogs. The other day one of them blew a brass horn as I passed. I do not know if he was calling something, or calling to other hunters that something (*pas moi!* I had hoped) was heading their way. The cheese rinds, egg shells, wilted lettuce, apple and pear cores, bits of old pâté that I have been trying to compost in the woods between my house and Château Montagne seem, instead, to be feeding Boris—my *nom de cochon* for a wild boar with an indiscriminate palate. Not that I have seen Boris, only that there are never any leavings from what I put out. Called to the hunter's horn or routed by their dogs, he would be good game—and no doubt a hearty ragout. Now that I have named him, I hope not. And he might be Borita.

A few days ago, a hunter brought a hind-quarter of deer to the family that has Molly. The *femme de la ferme* used her butcher knife to carve the evening meal—and then some. Two sheep dogs shared the bones. I was invited to stay. My host opened bottles from his best years.

"There was a saying on the Kansas frontier," I said by way of a toast, "that the men were so hungry when they came in from the roundups, that the women fed the dogs first." Having once worked on a small ranch in Kansas, I am known by the French as "Cueboy," and in that guise I am expected to offer bon mots from the American West. We raise our glasses.

A great storm of wind and rain has come and gone, and now it is clear—although I have learned by the French radio (I do not have television—or the Internet) that it will get *très froid*. So be it: I have wood, wool sweaters, and maybe Molly to keep me warm.

In the meantime, off to lunch today at the home of a painter friend where we will be joined by the widow of another painter friend. The afternoon will be a buzz of Bernard and Johns and Cassatt; as I know something about art, the talk among us will be a pleasure for me to recall—not unlike laying down bottles of good wine for a future of meals with friends. The most fruitful and natural play of the mind is conversation. I'll hold forth and dispute, but only for my own pleasure. *Tant pis* about death and all that.

I Have Not

Madame F., an eighty-year-old American ex-pat from California who lives beyond a line of poplars down the hill from me, fell leaving my house after dinner the other night and hurt herself badly: a nasty twisting of bones and cartilage in her left foot and lower leg. I got help from neighbors, and we took her to the hospital in Libourne. The French medical system is excellent; true, it is in a high fever of fiscal misery these days, but I sense the French think it is better to be in debt to themselves for their own care than to China for television sets, or to the Middle East for oil and war. After a few days, Madame was taken (not sent) home in a hospital van where medical attention continues: visits by a nurse a few times a week, and a doctor less often, but routinely—or as needed. Of course, there are her friends. Me among them.

In the mornings I start her wood stove, a long arrangement of cook ovens, griddle plates, burner tops and water reservoirs, that not only heats her old mill of a house but cooks the meals she makes for those of us who have been her guests. Evenings I walk her dog, Ginger, a tall Rhodesian Ridgeback who sits part way into the large fireplace in the evenings because, out of her country, she is cold.

My neighbor and I talk books: Russian stories we read together in the early fall, and now de Maupassant: *"Boule de Suif"* that made him famous; "The Story of a Farm Girl," and "Madame Tellier's Establishment." (We have agreed not to re-read "The Necklace" . . . in protest . . . but of what we are not sure.)

In between the Russians and the French, we confess our literary prejudices and affections: How much better Carlyle is as a writer on the French Revolution (even if wrong) than Dickens. The splendor of Chekhov. The recent death of Alain Robbe-Grillet and the novels of Duras (and while we are there, the wine by the same name). How neither of us have read Radiguet. All this and whatever comes from our mutual reading of the *Guardian* or *The New York Review of Books* (she subscribes to both), and *The New Yorker* (my subscription)—along with other literary journals and belles lettres magazines we share with one another, and with others in our circle.

The other evening she asked if I had met the *jeune fille Américaine* who this past summer moved into a farmhouse at

L'Etang on the Montagne estate; she is a painter. *Très belle.* I
have not. Madame confesses that she has asked her to do the
Monday morning market shopping. I am thanked for bringing in
wood from the sheds below the house and building and stoking
the fire, for walking Ginger—but the market needs a woman's
touch. And no doubt better French, not confusing *rougette* (a
small reddish lettuce) with *rouget* (a large reddish fish). Then
there was the matter of *aiguilles*, which I understood to be sewing needles but were, in the market patois, *aiguillettes*, thin strips
of meat; sewing needles cannot, as it turns out, be sautéed with
garlic in olive oil. Nor can lettuce be poached with lemon and
herbes de Provence.

Perhaps, Madame suggests, the three of us can read
Radiguet (in French) and talk about it over dinner one night. In
French.

I Am to Be a Godfather

It has been decided I am to be a godfather to Molly with visiting rights. It seems best she stay with the flock as she has made
friends with the other young lambs—three sets of twins among
them. That is fine by her, and by me. In the evenings, I prepare
her bottle, and when she hears me come out of the house into
which I first carried her, she bounds up the rows of vines to bleat
me a greeting. I know it is not love, but the bottle I carry, that is
love. French folk and flocks are not confused—or conflicted—
about such matters. We understand I will not take her home
but might, if the weather turns foul, carry her to the fireplace
where we first were father and daughter.

Tomorrow to the Saturday morning market in Sainte Foy
for myself, and to get a wedge of old Brebis (I can't make a
mistake about that) for my broken-footed friend. Cold tonight,

but good wood in my stove. Sans Molly, extra blankets. Maybe a nip of Armagnac. Maybe more than a nip.

Some Wines are at Home in a Pichet

My house sits at the carrefour of four wine districts. West is St. Emilion, one of the great regions of France. I have a few celebrated bottles that my friends gossip I am saving for my *lit de mort*. The younger French—mainly from the cities—think it is better to drink the good wines now, my prized St. Emilions included. I'll split the difference one winter night over a good cut of veal. And Saint Agru. Or maybe a meal with Madame when she is well enough to return to my table. That's it. The future is a promise you keep to yourself.

Across the Dordogne River (about ten kilometers south) is Entre-Duex-Mers—a light, white wine that I am told does not travel but is splendid here in summer. Or with *truite de mer* anytime. Crisp. Dry.

To the north a kilometer or two is Côtes des Francs. I can see the vines from my second floor windows. It is good wine and a good value. There is something tough and lean about it. In winter, it gets better if you open it and put the bottle by the wood stove thirty minutes before dinner. I drink half a bottle one night, then the other half the following night. Sometimes I fail at this arrangement.

The vines that surround my house are Côte de Castillon. It is those vines that produce Château Perreau Bel-Air, a wine I save for the few visitors from America I have these days. By looking out the French doors in my dining room cum office, they can see what they are drinking. Our toast is to tip our glasses to the grapes.

East five kilometers is Bergerac, a sturdy, dependable red wine. Monsieur R. resents the upscale vintners who are making Bergerac a Bordeaux-styled wine, so that it might be exported. "Some wines are at home in a pichet," he says. "'That way, 'if it gets broken at the table, desire shall not fail.' Confucius."

Monsieur is a chai of aphorisms. Roughly the age of Madame F., they are *chers amis*. He, too, is helping with her these days.

I don't catch Monsieur's meaning, but he seems pleased with himself for his saying, which he repeats, while he fills my jug. The wine—a mélange from his scattered small vineyards of various appellations—is strictly illegal, and that pleases him as well. One of his vineyards is not far from where the "Américaine Nouvelle"—as Monsieur calls her—lives. Between Madame F. and Monsieur R. her full name will become Mademoiselle Nouvelle Américaine.

"*Très nouvelle*," says Monsieur. " 'A young *tête sur les jeunes shoulders*,' to quote Catullus."

From time to time I have seen Mademoiselle Américaine driving the roads in a *très ancien* blue Dyna truck with potted flowers painted—by her?—on the doors. She zips by with such speed and apparent determination to get where she is going that I cannot get a good look at her. I doubt she sees me at all. Because I drive a maroon Deux Chevaux made by the same company and of about the same vintage, I thought one day to flash my lights as we passed: one *voiturette* to another. I got a quick flash in return. Next time I'll honk.

I say to Monsieur that all I remember from Catullus is, "what a woman says, you can write on the wind, write on the rushing waves."

"*Ah oui*," says Monsieur, "but wind and waves are lovely, and it is better to have a *faux récit* than *rien*. Far better, as Cicero says. And a man has well lived his life if he drinks the last bottle from his cellar on his last day," he continues as he corks my jug. Walking me to my Deux Chevaux he quotes Shakespeare that a young man should be whipped who plays at being a connoisseur of wine and sauces.

"It was Montaigne who said that about young men and wine," Madame told me when we were talking of Duras and Radiguet, "not Shakespeare. He gets many things wrong, and I think it is on purpose. Either that, or he is finally addled."

I ask her about the "broken pitcher at the table," and she believes it might be the Old Testament but is badly quoted and has nothing to do with wine. She'll look one day. I decide not to mention Cicero.

Many Shades of Gray

Gray is the color of the Dordogne sky this time of year. Many shades of gray. Sometimes with streaks of red or pink as the sun tries to burn its way through. The other day nothing got through because of a deep fog that came in the night. When I walked down to start Madame's fire the spider webs from summer were wisps of tendrils, white with the frozen frost. As I passed, they moved as if shivering. There was both the shade as well as the substance of things.

The grapevines and the wires on which they are strung were a dark brown, speckled with the white of the frozen fog. The grass in the pasture and the few large, round hay bales left from the fall mowing looked a pale yellow covered by a thin white shawl. Ten meters from my friend's house, I could only make out its shape: no doors, no windows. It will be the same for my house when I walk up the hill: only wizened webs in the icy air, and lines of brown vines making a perspective into the mist.

"Do you get fogs in Kansas?" Madame asks me as I load her stove.

I tell her not many, at least in the west where I lived. She is also curious about horizons. She understands that in Kansas you can see the edge of the earth in every direction. I tell her this is true.

"In California," she says, "you could see the edge of the earth in the sea. Here it is as if we do not have a horizon. At least I never think of it with all the trees and the hills."

She seems to study something in her mind, and I wonder if it is a recovered vision of the sea, or that she is imagining the vast sweep of High Plains pastures with its circle of horizons that is, for a moment, my own recovered vision.

When the fog cleared (two days' worth) it was such a lifting of gray that I saw the landscape as if for the first time. There were other, albeit muted, colors: dark evergreens among the brown and gray trees; trunks of the oaks and chestnuts with pale green-gray molds, and lichens up and down their barks; in the winter's pale light, moss is everywhere on the rocks and trees—not just on the north side as it is in Kansas. With evening, the tree trunks and the tree limbs grow a Manet black before all else.

Large dark green balls with dots of white (like Christmas decorations) appear in the trees after the leaves have fallen: mistletoe. It is not prized by the French but is by the English who live in the area. High in the tall trees, it is difficult to get. When I was a college student I saw similar balls of mistletoe, also out of reach high in the trees. I made Christmas money one year by shooting into them with a .22 rifle so that they splintered and I could collect the stems and berries when they fell. It is not a trick I am going to teach the French hunters.

I had a friend in those days who made wreaths of the mistletoe by adding greens and holly berries that she gathered from the woods. We sold the wreaths to the professors' wives and spent the money on books not required for our classes. And for a case of wine we shared, my first and hers, as well: Château Lafleur. I still have a bottle, empty to be sure. And a small volume of Montaigne, still full.

Charlie Brown's Snoopy Fighting the Red Baron

I am a father again: Noel, a ram this time, lost his mother
a few days after she gave birth. Sometimes the ewes in this
country die mysteriously, perhaps of a calcium deficiency,
and we think that is what happened. Noel, like Molly, is
now bottle fed three times a day. Two orphans together, we
wonder if they will become friends as they run to the farmhouse side by side to get their meals. Molly seems to bleat
more; Noel is the serious one. As a parent, I should not have
favorites. Molly is my favorite.

Cold and damp in recent days. Cold is cold. Damp is damp.
In the Dordogne, they add up to more than Cold and Damp.
Because the bottom half of my house is built into a hillside
it does not get warm in winter. My wood stove is in the fireplace upstairs, as is (thankfully) the bathtub. Only the kitch-
en and the dining room are downstairs. It is where I type,
in my red stocking hat and white scarf—a vision of Charlie
Brown's Snoopy fighting the Red Baron, should a blue
voiturette stop by now that we have flashed one another.

I might go to Paris for a few days to see friends. Paris is what
makes me an American writer, and I need to visit it now and
then to make sure it is still there. And I am still there as well.

I Am a Man of a Certain Age

Madame asks what I will be writing. She is discreet enough
not to ask what I am writing. Verb tenses matter in matters of
literary decorum.

For lunch we are having *soupe eternelle*. At the Monday market I had bought a sturdy, wood-fired dark bread. If kept in a box

in a cold room, it will last the week. In addition to the bread and soup there is the *vieux brebis* from Sainte Foy and a *pichet* of *vin rouge* from Monsieur R. Ginger is partway in the fireplace. Anna, Madame's cat, is curled on a wicker chair. I am at the stove.

"You don't need to say about your writing," she says. "If you are *superstitieux*."

My friend is trying to improve my French, and she does this not only by using words I do not know, but cognates as well. In this way she is an excellent teacher; there are days when I walk home with a new word in my head, repeating it as I go, until I get back to my Mansion's French/English Dictionary from my student days.

Pinceau, pinceau, pinceau, I said to the vines the other day after Madame and I had had a long talk about Piero Della Francesca: *Pinceau, pinceau,* up the hill I talked and walked and talked until, settled by my wood stove, I found on page 471 it had been a "paint brush" that the vignobles had heard on my way past them—and that a phrase I had misplaced along the way was waiting on the same page: *coup de pinceau,* the stroke of the paint brush. Piero Della Francesca, we had observed the hour before, has lovely ones.

I tell Madame I am not *superstitieux*, and that in answer to her question, one day I am going to write a story—maybe a long story *á la de* Maupassant—that is *méditatif*. A *récit méditatif*.

"Will it have dialogue?" she asks.

Not much, I say. It will be composed like a Montaigne essay, but it will be fiction. I will use his aphorisms, but not put them in italics. There would be no plot.

"*Pas d'intrigue!*" Madame says in mock alarm. "Will anyone in America read such a story? *Pas du tout!*" She smiles as I bring the soup to the table and pour the wine. I decide not to tell her I am indeed *superstitieux*—but not about what she has asked, or how she has asked. I touch wood as I put down the soup.

"*Soupe eternelle, c'est moi,*" says Madame. "*Et toi.*" It is her traditional toast over her traditional soup. We tip our glasses toward one another. She seems amused that I could write a story bereft of readers. Delicious pleasures when enjoyed by themselves don't need the world's touch.

"The soup," she says as we start our meal, "has a *supplémentaire* by Mademoiselle Américaine. She was here yesterday."

It is a rich soup: beans and rice, mixed with bits of both rabbit and chicken. It is pleasing enough, Madame and I think, to warrant a second glass of wine. And more bread to mop the plates clean.

"You should put French words into your *récit méditatif,*" Madame says. "Add a phrase or two: *et peu à peu,* and you will get the language. And in this way your book will make you."

I walk off lunch on my way to Molly's, sensing snow in the air. When I get there, I rack the stove wood cut from the previous day, then cut long logs and stack them like tepee poles around straight trees. That done, Molly and Noel are to be fed (they remind me in not-so-subtle ways) before all is dusk, then dark. I am invited to stay for dinner but decline. I have a dish of my own making at home: a casserole of potatoes, carrots, onions, and *saucisse de canard* into which I stir (a secret) my unique Moutarde Douce sauce. There is also a glass of *eau de vie de prune* I have promised myself for some reason I will fabricate along the way: Better a *faux raison* than none.

As I walk along, the scent of snow becomes snow itself. I am to stop at Madame's to stoke her stove for the night. Getting there I see the blue Dyna in her driveway, and I see Mademoiselle walking toward the house: tall, a holly berry scarf around her neck. Black peacoat, its collar turned up. Jeans. Long legs. Yellow stocking cap. As she goes in the door, the light from inside shines on her face. She is young. Half my years. I am a man of a certain age.

A puff of smoke comes from Madame's chimney, and I know all inside is well and warm. Before I head up the hill home, I study in the dim light the potted flowers painted on the side of Mademoiselle's truck: a mixture of geraniums, deep purple petunias, bright-eyed pansies, and a tiny orange flower I do not know. Cold as it is, there is a sturdy glow to them. "Audacious," I think, both the flowers to be out in the winter night, and to paint them on the side of the old truck. Audacious: I'll look it up.

Monsieur R.

Monsieur R. is French, but lived a number of years in California where he worked in the movie business, and so speaks excellent English. However, we have agreed to speak French in order that mine might improve.

But Monsieur's French occasionally slips into a stream of French and English, unbroken, as if he is speaking an integrated language, a patois that is richer and more fluent than mere Franglais. He seems not to notice this. Madame tells me he speaks that way to her as well, and the times he has joined us for a meal, I observe this is true.

Monsieur is also given to asserting the truth of matters that are not, strictly speaking, true. The other day, as he was drawing my four liters of his vin rouge plus another five liters for Madame, he announced (apropos of nothing I could fathom) that "Jesus said casseroles should *pas* call kettles *noirs*." And later, in the same conversation, he quoted Montaigne that a man needs six hours sleep, a woman seven, while a fool takes eight.

"You should hear what he does in the name of Cervantes and Brillat Saverin," Madame says when I stop by with her wine.

"'A meal that does not end with cheese is like a pretty woman with a mustache.' It is not a mustache but with one eye, and it was not Sancho who said it, but Brillat Saverin who wrote it. Oh well," she says with a laugh. "And the way he quotes you!"

Me? I ask.

"Yes," she says. "And me as well. We are all persona in his *oeuvre*."

Me? I ask again.

"Ah oui!" she says. "You have *une histoire à la* Monsieur. Complete with intrigue and dialogue. And aphorisms. The other day he had you saying there is no Royal road to learning, which I think comes from Dickens or Trollope."

I said I remembered saying no such thing, but that I was pleased to be credited.

"He quotes me as saying 'far-fetched and dear bought is not good for women,' which comes from where I don't know, but not from me," says Madame. "And he quoted Mademoiselle Américaine saying art is long but life is short, which she might have said because it is an old saying; at least I have heard it before. Still it is not what someone young would say. And, I don't think they have even met. But soon she, too, will have *an histoire*. No doubt entangled with yours. He is trying to decide if he will have you returning to what he calls black-and-white Kansas when spring comes, or if you are staying here in technicolor France. It is some reference from his movie days. You are in more than a *récit méditatif*, I assure you."

I am at Madame's sink bottling her wine when I notice something new over the fireplace: her portrait. Acrylic, I think. A pale gold background that sets off her white hair and against which her face is luminous. Her head is tilted right to left against the traditional line. Her eyes are rendered large and dark brown, but not enough to be piercing. The painting is beautifully composed and rich with under-painting. Madame is lovely in it, although likeness was probably not the object of the artist.

"I have no wrinkles," Madame says, when she finds me looking at it. "She put Botox on her palette. Her *coups de pinceau* are unique—'*Seul en son genre.*' The same as in the potted flowers on the side of her truck. I like especially the orange Million Bells because they are from pots of mine. Have you seen the flowers on her truck?"

I say I have: *Intrépide.*

"*Ah oui,*" says Madame and smiles at my new word.

Vin Included

If I go to Paris, it will be from the train station in Castillon, the small market town where on Mondays I buy my fish and from-age and, from the tall Madagascar woman, the wood-fired bread that lasts a week.

After shopping, I take a *grande crème* at the Commerce Cafe with friends, also there for the Monday market. We gossip—mostly in English to accommodate my poor French—about the usual: weather, grapes, the price of gas, and the good lunches to be had next door at the Hôtel des Voyageurs, the home of Yu-Yu, a small parrot that does not like anybody very much and me, it seems, in particular: always squawking with grating intensity when I come in.

"Before Yu-Yu there was Mal-Mal," says Monsieur R. "He had excellent French profanity. Some very good words."

The Hôtel des Voyageurs is a Ticket Restaurant. In Castillon there are no Michelin stars, no Rotand Walking Men stickers. A Ticket sign on the door means it is for those who work in town and do not want to go home for lunch. In that case, their employer has made an arrangement for a meal: If you come back over and over again—a kind of *habitué*—I think you earn a discount on a future meal, or maybe the meal itself. I am not all that sure how it works. I should ask. Now that I think of it, I have seen such restaurants in Paris. At the Hôtel des Voyageurs you can get a three-course meal for eight euros. Vin included.

The restaurant has two rooms, divided by the kitchen in which there is a fireplace, used as a grill. The old vine stumps (*pieds de vignes*) that are pulled each winter from the vineyard below my house (and others all along the *côte*) are bundled and sold for fire wood. There are mathematical odds *à la* Diderot that the *côte de porc* I ate for lunch at the Hôtel des Voyageurs the other day had been cooked over the pieds that made the wine that was included in the meal.

As for the room behind the kitchen: I am not allowed. Once when I looked, it was packed with men eating *ensemble* at a long broad wooden table. They were pouring the dregs of their wine into the dregs of their soup and drinking it out of the bowls; crusts of bread were scattered about, the men's spoons and forks making a *porte couteau* of them. From the front room we heard the swarthy laughter of these men. I am not sure women are allowed. I am pretty sure they are not.

I have decided: In a few days I will ride my two-horse, maroon Deux Chevaux to the train station in Castillon, park it, and go to Paris.

What Rat?

"Does she ask you to pee in her compost?" says Monsieur R. We have arrived by chance at the same time to do chores for Madame and are walking her lane toward the house. Before I can answer, Monsieur says: "Every cock will crow upon his own dunghill."

For a moment in my mind's eye I see him taking a pee on Madame's compost while crowing away. The vision passes and I say, no, she has not made such a request, although she has asked me to continue her compost while she is unable—a small square plot fenced off against Boris, should he get tired of my fare.

"Nor me," says Monsieur. "But Burton in his *Melancholy* writes that peeing into the compost makes it richer."

Monsieur is a tall man with large hands and long arms. He is older than I am, but the bounce in his stride is younger than mine. There is a movie-actor visage about him; something beyond handsome or distinguished. No doubt he has broken many hearts.

"And what shall we do with the rat?" he asks. We are at the door, and, without knocking, Monsieur walks in—not waiting for an answer from me, which would have been: *quel rat?*

Monsieur has come this day to make croutons out of the bits of Madame's bread leftover from last week, including the forked ends of the baguettes serpentines she has me buy. He takes great care in making his croutons, using sea salt, good garlic, and Spanish olive oil he gets from a friend near Seville who, Madame confides, may or may not be a woman. *Un peu d' intrigue.*

"And we do not know for sure if he is married as he claims to be," Madame has said. "I have never seen a wife. First, she was in California; then she is in Greece with her dying mother; recently she has come and gone from London. She is in Paris. She is in Belgrade. She is with a friend in Addis Ababa. I think Monsieur R. only says he is married so he won't be pressed to marry. This has been going on for years—even before he returned from California. I would not marry him if he asked, so he has nothing to fear from me. And Countess P. will not have him in her house, so he need not worry about her."

It is Countess P. who lives in Montagne with—or without—broken fingers. I have never seen her, although it is said she drives out now and again.

I had wondered why there always seemed to be a large bowl of croutons on the kitchen counter. And when I thought of it, I should have wondered about other dishes that seemed to appear: Who had made the potage Crécy or the *saucisson* with horseradish sauce? Or the potage *bonne femme* (which became the base of my own *soupe eternelle*, now in weak competition with the Mademoiselle Américaine's version). And who was leaving lovely apple tarts with thin, delicate crusts?

"What is to be done with the rat?" says Monsieur from the counter where he is mixing the stale bread chunks in the iron skillet with its hot Spanish olive oil, garlic, sea salt, and a concoction of spices.

"I think it best to take him to the Dordogne," says Madame. "Is he caught?" They are talking about a Ragundin rat for whom Madame had set a trap by her pond before she fell.

"He is not," says Monsieur. "But when he is, let me drown him in the trap. I take him to the Dordogne and he returns and you catch him again; then, I take him to the Dordogne and he comes back. Voltaire writes that 'man is born free but that everywhere he is like a rat in a trap.'"

"You have it wrong," says Madame from her wheel chair. "It is 'that everywhere he is in chains: *dans les fers.*' And it was Rousseau, not Voltaire."

"I take it," says Monsieur (and here he uses Madame's pet name at which she blushes so that he smiles with the youth that is in his walk), "you would rather not have us say: 'How now! A Rat? Dead for farthing.' And yes, he is caught."

"It's Shakespeare," she says, "and I doubt it's a farthing. But I thought you said the rat has not been caught."

"What difference does verb tense make?" says Monsieur. "'Will be caught,' 'has been caught,' 'is caught,' 'shall be caught.' Since the war and Camus, we are all '*aujourd'hui c'est moi qui suis mort.*' *Et le* rat, also!"

"No," says Madame (and here she uses a pet name for Monsieur R. at which he smiles toward me), "I do not want him dead. To the Dordogne. Swim, swim, vile rat, swim. And you don't know for sure the same rat returns."

"I'll paint him," Monsieur retorts. "Polka dots of orange water-resistant paint from a spray can I have in my truck. If Monsieur Ragundin comes back, we will know. Then, Madame," and here he turns off his frying pan and scatters his croutons on a paper towel, "will you let me drown him? He would make excellent fertilizer for your tomato plants. I will cut him into pieces and put one piece per plant: a hindquarter here, the *tête* there, the butt end here. The innards there. A big Ragundin will be food for a dozen tomato plants that will produce sixty round, red, grosse tomatoes with ease."

"The tomatoes will smell like rat."

"No more than your onions smell like pee."

"A dead rat stinks more than a live man's pee," she says.

"That's Ovid. Ovid says that."

"He did not," she says. "I said that."

"Well, then," Monsieur says, bringing his croutons to the table so we can taste test them, "let us talk about Countess P's. tongue."

"What about her tongue?" says Madame.
"How the tip of it was cut off to get the keys to her safe and now she talks gibberish."

I Never Fail to Touch It

From the Castillon gare, the local train goes first to Libourne—a large wine center of a city—where I catch the TGV to Paris. Three and a half hours later I am at Gare Montparnasse. I stay at a small hotel not that far from where Gertrude Stein had her salon.

I have friends in Paris, among them Jane and her husband, Jean Louis, who join me for lunch at Balzar near the Sorbonne. Years ago we saw Barbra Streisand and her husband, James Brolin, eating at a table against the wall. Jane noticed the husband who, I was told, is a "hunk" (no French translation possible, unless Mr. Brolin is a hunk of cheese: In that case he is a *gros morceau*, which he is probably not).

After lunch I walked past the nearby bronze statue of Montaigne, his legs crossed with his right shoe sticking out tempting the students to touch it for good luck. Over the years it has lost its patina and is now a very shiny shoe indeed. I never fail to touch it.

I am also friends with a short-story writer of New Yorker fame, Madame G. We met years ago at Reclaimer, the restaurant where she had fed one of her characters. I ordered the meal of her story. Madame G. smiled.

These days I have been walking through cemeteries. I made my way to Père Lachaise and, for a populist friend in Kansas, stood against the wall where the members of the Paris Commune were shot. Nearby, I put my hand on the stone of Oscar Wilde because we share a birthday and because I like the remark attributed to him as he lay dying in a Paris hotel: Either the wallpaper goes or I do.

Other days I walk as I always do: in no particular direction except along the rues I have walked before. The bloom of novelty has given way to the autumn of the familiar. I like to see where I have been, and where I have lived: Place Dauphine, rue Xavier Prévis (where I once rented an apartment above a couscous restaurant, but not so far above that Boris-sized cockroaches were put off by the climb). I use the Pont des Arts whenever I cross the Seine.

One sunny summer day a few years ago I came upon two students—a young man and a young woman—standing by the railing of the bridge in rain coats; a third student (I supposed they were all students; they had that look about them of going for pleasure to get their profit) collected money in a hat—all the while checking for the police. When the hat was full (I put in a euro not knowing to what I was contributing) the young man and woman began laughing, then stripped off their raincoats and, to a "standing" ovation, dove naked into the Seine. Their business associate ran down along the quais with the rain coats and the money as they swam ashore. No gendarmes out of Truffaut arrived, whistles blowing.

Before my train departed for the return trip to Libourne, I spent an hour walking through cimetière Montparnasse. Just inside the gate are Sartre and Simone de Beauvoir; some way in, and with the help of a small map you get at the entrance, I found Man Ray. I have always admired his photograph of Gertrude and Alice with the paintings as a backdrop. I found the stone of Samuel Beckett and sat there for a moment, waiting.

After three days—and a meal at Closerie des Lilas as a guest of prosperous friends—I returned. It was Sunday and the oyster market was open in Castillon; I bought a dozen number two Arcachons. In my refrigerator was a split of Gremillet: cold and crisp. I steamed the oysters in vin blanc and water until they opened. Some cheese and red wine and bread in front of my wood stove, and then, as Pepys says: So to bed.

The next afternoon when I go to the farm, I learn that Molly does not exactly remember me (how quickly they forget), but Noel does. And there is Sylvester. Sylvester? Yes. He was born (perhaps while I was waiting on Samuel Beckett) and his mother will have nothing to do with him: So now there are three. Bleats all around. And well, yes, Molly does remember me. Or something about me.

"Hello," says a tall young woman as I return to the kitchen carrying three empty milk bottles.

My Cork Basket is Half Empty

I am more than halfway through winter. I know because the basket where I keep old corks is much depleted. There are many clocks that mark the seasons in the Dordogne. These days you can see the vineyard owners planting new vines. The shooting from hunters has stopped. Primrose is blooming. Paperwhites are for sale in the markets. The daffodils that were planted up against the stone walls of the old houses and barns where the ground is warmer are coming up. V's of cranes are heading north. The wild plum trees between me and Montagne are starting into bloom. And my cork basket is half empty.

I use the corks to start my wood stove. When I open a new bottle I try not to pierce the cork so that I can turn it around for the wine I bottle from my jug. There is a curious pleasure in pulling a cork from a fine St. Emilion (only a few of these) from an appellation de R, illegal, and bare of label. Twice pierced, the corks can no longer be used for bottling but have other jobs; "double tasking," I have learned it is now called in America.

"Triple tasking," now that I think of it. And tant pis for the prohibition against new wine in old bottles.

I save the spring-through-fall corks for winter fires. They are splendid starters (candle stubs are good as well) if you stuff a few in crumpled newspaper: I use the *International Herald Tribune* or, if I am feeling pretentiously French, *Le Monde*. Once the corks catch, they burn with great brilliance and flame. And kindle the wood into warmth.

The French Make Terrible Fences

The farmer with Molly, Noel, and Sylvester has asked me to cut fence posts out of his woods. He, too, knows that spring is coming and his demand for firewood is not as great, but he will need fence posts for a new corral I am to build around the sheep shed. The French make terrible fences. Not even the most hardscrabble Kansas ranch has such awful fences as most of the farms in France have. Both the posts (twisted and tilted) and the fence itself (drooping wires) are badly done. The gates are a wobbly wreck. They don't know how to make a brace post or set a dead man. They don't see the need to make the gate posts bigger than fence posts.

If there are not more pressing chores, I will show the owner how to build a proper fence. But it won't be easy. There are no fence stretchers to be bought or borrowed; the French fence wire is thin and of poor quality. They use bent nails for staples. But we'll see. In the meantime I am cutting the posts, plus extra wood for the fireplace should spring be false. For sure, I am going to build a sturdy and straight-lined corral, stout enough to hold a High Plains Gomer bull.

Yesterday from the woods where I was working, I watched Mademoiselle drive up to the farmhouse and go in. She was wearing a bulky white sweater and the same stocking cap and maroon scarf as when I first saw her.

I turned off the chainsaw and thought to join her now that we have met, if briefly ("I'm sorry, I must be going," she had said. "An errand to run for Madame." And out the door she went).

I am not shy. I talk a good game. But something—not being covered with wood chips nor that I no doubt reeked of work—stopped me.

No Dénouement

"And will there be a gun over the fireplace to go off before the end?"

Madame is again curious about what I will be writing. I tell her there will be fireplaces, large enough for cold dogs to sit by on winter days, but no guns over them.

We have been reading Chekhov: Yalta is warmer than the Dordogne this time of year. The pleasure in reading Chekhov is in rereading him. There is no story we plan to boycott. Monsieur R. wants us to read *King Lear,* but Madame has resisted.

"He thinks the play is funny," she said. "However, what he quotes from it is accurate—at least by my memory. The other day he was here saying that 'age is unnecessary,' and sure enough, after he left, I found it. I suppose that is amusing in a way, but I am not in a good enough mood to be amused by *King Lear.*"

It occurs to me that Monsieur R. has never asked what I do or why I am living here. When first we met, he seemed to assume I had been in my small house on the hill for as long as he had been in his assortment of stone barns and buildings and chais. Or as long as Madame in her converted mill. And further, it was as if we had all been in California together, whenever that was. Not that I know that Monsieur and Madame knew one another in California, but there was that remark she made about Monsieur's *faux femme* in California. I am shy to ask.

It is also true that Madame has never asked what brought me here, or why I have stayed. Or why I am alone. She may be shy to ask. I think this is true.

"Will there be a curtain that bangs?" asks Madame.

I say there will not be a curtain. A scrim only. Through which the *intrépide* reader can see.

"But *dénouement?* There must be a *dénouement.*"

We are waiting for Monsieur to join us for dinner, and—perhaps—Mademoiselle, although that invitation by Madame has not been unconditionally accepted, something about getting to Bordeaux and back in search of art supplies.

From the stove where I am fixing the meal, I say to Madame that since there will be no raveling, there will be no unraveling. *Pas de dénouement.* However, "age will be necessary." She cannot help herself now and smiles. We hear someone has arrived. "And some things will be left not said, or explained," she says as Ginger goes to the door to see who has come.

"*Ah oui,*" I say.

Francis Bacon

Monsieur has asked if I am married. I tell him I am not. He has finished filling my jug and Madame's as well. Outside it is raining: drip, drip, drip, as Dickens would write to earn his penny a word. It has been too warm in recent days to start the wood stoves for the few evenings that it is damp and cold. I do, however, keep Madame's fireplace going. It cheers her, I think, to sit by it with Anna in her lap and Ginger toasting herself first on one side then the other.

"All was not merry as a marriage bell?" Monsieur says, his voice half a question. I am trying to guess if it is one of his quotations. But before I can ask, he says: "Madame used to be married and now she is not: 'Hush, hark, a deep sound strikes like a rising knell.'" He is quiet for a moment. "Byron," he says.

"And you?" I find myself having the nerve to ask. "Are you married?"

"There is a story I am," he says. He smiles the way he did when he used Madame's pet name. Then putting his arm around the side of the vat out of which he has just drawn the wine he says: "Which wife is this? The one I adored first and so took a second, or the other the other way around?"

"Oscar Wilde," I say.

Monsieur looks at me for a moment as if to drop a mask. Then he says:

"When I was a boy, I worked in the Montaigne vineyards. One day the owner gave me a book of quotations in English that a guest had given him. He knew I wanted to learn the language. Before that, I had no English. Each night when I came home, I would study the book. I set myself a goal to learn three quotations a day and say them out loud as I was working in the vineyards. It was only later that I would get the meanings. After I understood what I was saying, I would only learn the quotations I liked. Nobody knew what I was saying, so I was talking to myself, and after awhile I would have one of me say a quotation to the other of me, and the second me would answer in a quotation. For two years I did this."

I realize Monsieur has answered a question I did not ask, and not answered the one I did. I am charmed by this evasion, if that is what it is—and it is probably not.

From a bin behind the vat he fetches a bottle, checks its cork and its punt, which I can see is deep. It has no label.

"Here," he says. "There is a story in this wine. It is yours for the drinking and telling."

I thank him. Looking at the bottle, I say that we are of an age when old wood is best to burn, old authors best to read, and old wine best to drink.

"I don't know it," he says. "But now I do. I assign it to Bacon."

Today I Told a White Lie That Helped

Madame is getting restless. Over the years she has been the epitome of independence, and it vexes her not to be so now. The doctor says she will be walking on her own in a few weeks (it has been two months since she fell), but she doesn't quite believe it. Monsieur tells her Virgil says we do the most damage to ourselves by impatience.

"It comes from Montaigne," she says to me. "I don't think he ever gets any of them right, and I wonder if once upon a time he knew better and just set about to test and tease me, but by now he has forgotten that was his purpose, and has it in his head as fact that it was Virgil. And that you said 'Never trust the writer; trust the tale.'"

I smile and she knows I said no such thing.

"He is Google itself," she says.

I ask how she knows about Google—as I don't know much about it, only that it exists. She says the same, then adds:

"I understand you can find what you want to know in an instant, and that seems to me a bad way to go about the life of the mind, as if knowing something in an instant will lead to knowledge, much less to wisdom. Where is the pleasure of serendipity? And of friends who read as we do. I don't drink instant coffee. I don't make instant tea. Or minute rice. I make *soupe eternelle*. There is more than a difference."

She seems gloomy at the thought of Google. I have been teasing her about one thing or another in the past few days to bring her cheer, but that is wearing thin. She knows her flowers are starting up and the garden needs tending. We all help as we can, but not much will lift her spirits until she can get around pretty much by herself.

Today I tell a white lie that helped. I say the fishmonger at the Monday market had asked after her; she likes the fish-monger, a broad-faced, large-shouldered man who juggles lemons at his stand in between customers. In fact, it had been the flat-nosed egg woman (whom she doesn't like). Anyway, what's a fib good for, if not to bring on a smile. At the ranch where I worked in Kansas, they were called "right lies," some mishearing passed down through the generations.

"Tell the fishmonger," says Madame, "that I will return when I can walk on my own through the market, and that we shall have champagne and snails for lunch at the Hôtel des Voyageurs to celebrate. He will be charmed to know we can turn *boudin* and *vin de table* into escargot and champagne.

"As will Monsieur R." I say.

"It is where I got the menu," she says. "Only he claims such a menu is there, and after we have not had it, we will have had it. I know this to be true in advance of it being so." Now, I am the one who smiles.

Someone is at Madame's door.

A Recovered Vision in Place of a Dénouement

If I stay in this country, will I stir fact into fiction? Have others say for me what I cannot say so well for myself? Will *soupe eternelle* be the life of my mind, and intrigue find me—but not in an instant? Will I learn my *histoire*? And will it have neither raveling nor unraveling? Will I be as *intrépide* as flowers on the side of an old truck? Will blood sausage and table wine become snails and champagne one Monday in a Ticket restaurant with a parrot that does not like me?

Or is the story for the telling in Monsieur's wine bottle that I return to a recovered vision of black-and-white Kansas where moss is only on the north side of the trees and rocks. Where we build fences with good wire, and stout corrals with strong gates. Where we feed the dogs first and know why we set dead men.

Looking at the great sweep of pastures and horizons that stretch to the edge of the earth in all directions, do I believe it myself?

Someone is at my door.